Praise for *From A to X*

"Berger's work feels wrought with a miniaturist's precision, a quality of gravely considered intimacy that might be taken for tenderness … Persistently, sometimes insistently, he calls us back to an awareness of form, of invention, and through these to an awareness of the world in which we sit turning his pages – the world and all its exigencies."

– Leah Hager Cohen, *New York Times*

"John Berger has found a voice perfectly fitted to express an emotional sincerity quite rare in fiction at the moment."

– Ursula K. Le Guin, *Guardian*

"A soaring romance of heroic virtue and true love."

– *Evening Standard*

"This little book is magic, evoked through the voice of a woman intent on making the best of a difficult situation. It is original and graceful, sustained by a quiet rage … this most original of artists has yet again looked to the profound in the ordinary … a narrative possessing the passion of a love song, the vision of a seer and the anger of a militant."

– Eileen Battersby, *Irish Times*

"Superb passages of writing take on a gripping physicality and a corresponding profundity." – *Financial Times*

"Encompasses moments of rare poignancy." – *Sunday Telegraph*

"Dazzling … worthy of Nabokov or Defoe … *From A to X* is told in the passionate, unwavering voice of a lover who has accepted separation in body but not in spirit. A mixture of two of the world's most universal narratives, love and resistance, this short novel carries the scent of rose-water and the punch of tear gas."

– Michael Lukas, *San Francisco Chronicle*

"At its finest, which is very fine indeed, there's a rawness, an impatience under the perfectly cadenced words." – *Scotsman*

"Wonderfully profound, containing the same kind of poetry as Primo Levi's *The Periodic Table*." – *Time Out*

"The same novelist who wrote *G.*, still passionate about justice and equality, remains at his post, recording these desperate lives, their struggle for freedom, and honouring their endeavour."
– Patricia Duncker, *Literary Review*

"A rich narrative . . . a paean to protest, both political and romantic."
– *Publishers Weekly*

"John Berger has given us an exquisite thing. This is a book of controlled rage sculpted with tools of tenderness and a searing political vision. Everything he writes about is profound, precise and invoiced: Liberty and the lack of it, hope and the lack of it, love and the terrible yearning that takes its place when the loved one has been taken away."
– Arundhati Roy

"Berger's writing is as strong and passionate as ever … a heartrending love story and a searing indictment of authoritarianism in all its forms … This is a beautiful, poetic hymn to the human spirit that will live long in the minds of all who read it." –*New Internationalist*

"As many levels as this novel has … it ultimately folds back into its own overflowing heart. What are messages between lovers but the invention of a shared, secret world? A'ida and Xavier ache to be together. The two life sentences he is serving may not be consecutive; one is his and one is hers." – *Los Angeles Times*

"Berger, a writer of conscience, exquisite restraint, and tender sensuality, tells a beautifully sorrowful story of love, conviction, and defiance in a time of brutal indifference." – *Booklist*

ALSO BY JOHN BERGER

A Painter of Our Time
Permanent Red
The Foot of Clive
Corker's Freedom
A Fortunate Man
Art and Revolution
The Moment of Cubism and Other Essays
The Look of Things: Selected Essays and Articles
Ways of Seeing
Another Way of Telling
A Seventh Man
G.
About Looking
Into Their Labours: A Trilogy
(Pig Earth, Once in Europa, Lilac and Flag)
And Our Faces, My Heart, Brief as Photos
The Sense of Sight
The Success and Failure of Picasso
Keeping a Rendezvous
Pages of the Wound
Photocopies
To the Wedding
King
The Shape of a Pocket
Titian: Nymph and Shepherd
(with Katya Berger)
Selected Essays
Here Is Where We Meet
Hold Everything Dear

Storyteller, novelist, essayist, screenwriter, dramatist and critic, **John Berger** is one of the most internationally influential writers of the last fifty years. His many books include *Ways of Seeing*, the fiction trilogy *Into Their Labours*, *Here Is Where We Meet*, the Booker Prize–winning novel *G*, and, most recently, *Hold Everything Dear*.

From A *to* X

A Story in Letters
by John Berger

VERSO
London • New York

First published by Verso 2008
This paperback edition published by Verso 2009

3 5 7 9 10 8 6 4 2

Verso
UK: 6 Meard Street, London W1F 0EG
USA: 20 Jay Street, Suite 1010, Brooklyn, NY 11201
www.versobooks.com

Verso is the imprint of New Left Books

ISBN-13: 978-1-84467-361-2

British Library Cataloguing in Publication Data
A catalogue record for this book is available from the British Library

Library of Congress Cataloging-in-Publication Data
A catalog record for this book is available from the Library of Congress

Typeset in Janson by Hewer Text UK Ltd, Edinburgh
Printed in the United States

For

DONK, BEV and SUNSHINE

and in memory of

GHASSAN KANAFANI

Love is not time's fool . . .
Love alters not with his brief hours and weeks
But bears it out even to the edge of doom.

If this be error, and upon me prov'd
I never writ, nor no man ever lov'd.

Shakespeare, Sonnet 116.

Some letters recuperated by John Berger

Last year when the new high-security prison built on the hills to the north of the town of Suse was opened, the old prison in the town centre was shut down and abandoned.

The last occupant of cell no. 73 in the old prison had arranged against the wall where the regulation bunk was, a shelf of pigeonholes. He had constructed it out of empty Marlboro cigarette cartons and attached it solidly to the wall with Scotch tape. Each pigeonhole was large enough for several decks of cards. In three of them some packets of letters were found.

Such daylight as entered the cell came through a small round opening, out of reach, at the top of one wall. The cell measured 2.5m x 3m and was 4m high.

A long corridor with barred windows and opaque glass connected the cells in this wing of the old prison to a communal hall which was like a bunker, with primitive cooking facilities, a water tap, a TV, benches, tables and a raised platform for the permanent armed guards.

The last prisoner in cell no. 73, accused of being a founder member of a terrorist network, and serving two life sentences, was known as Xavier. The letters found in the pigeonholes were addressed to him.

It becomes clear on reading them that the letters were not arranged in chronological order. A'ida – if this is her real name – did not date her letters with the year, only with the day of the month. It's clear that the correspondence continued over a good many years. Rather than trying by deduction or guesswork to re-establish their chronological order, R. and I, as we transcribed them, decided to respect the order in which they had been arranged by Xavier. Sometimes on the back of the pages of A'ida's letters (she never wrote on both sides of the paper) Xavier made notes. These too we transcribed and they are printed in this book in *a more muted typeface.*

A'ida obviously chose not to refer in her letters to her ongoing life as an activist. Occasionally, however, she couldn't resist what I suspect to be a reference. This is how I interpret her remarks about playing canasta. I doubt whether she played canasta. Following the same prudence, she surely changed the names of close acquaintances, as well as place names. Since A'ida and Xavier were not married there was no possibility of her obtaining permission to visit him.

There are a few letters which A'ida wrote and did not send. Sometimes, it seems, she began a letter knowing from the start that it was not one she would post; on other occasions the rush of what she had to say led her to write things which on reflection she decided it was better to keep.

How the unsent and sent letters came into my possession must remain, for the moment, a secret, for the explanation would endanger other parties.

The unsent letters are written on the same blue paper as the sent ones. I have placed them in the packets where it seemed to me they fitted. But you can change them.

Wherever Xavier and A'ida are today, dead or alive, may God keep their shadows.

J.B.

The First Packet of Letters

On the strip of cotton fabric that ties together the packet, are the following words, written in an ink that the cloth has somewhat blotted:

The universe resembles a brain, not a machine. Life is a story being told now. The first reality is story. This is what being a mechanic has taught me.

My On-the-ground-lion,

Did you receive my last parcel? In it I put Marlboros, Zambrano, green mint, coffee.

When I awoke today it was blue sky. I could hear the braying of a donkey far away, and, much nearer, the rustling noise of a shovel turning cement, interspersed with knocks against the earth to make the cement slide off it. Dimitri is building another room on to his house. I lay there thinking lazily of my body and how it sidles without me, for I knew I didn't have to be at the pharmacy until 9.30 am. I lay in bed, my right hand touching my groin. I tell you this so you can picture me. Nobody can prevent you.

How is your foot? Is it healing?

Your A'ida

P.S.

Saw a chameleon yesterday, he was climbing down a tree trunk on to the ground. The way they can twist their pelvises – their very small pelvises have iliac crests like ours but they swivel differently on the backbone – is comic and handy. They can plant their weight, at the same moment, on a vertical wall and a horizontal floor! For negotiating certain difficulties we might learn from them, don't you think? According to Alexis, chameleon means in Greek *On-the-ground-lion.*

1,000 million people do not have access to drinking water. In some areas of Brazil 1 litre of drinking water costs more to buy on the street than 1 litre of milk, in Venezuela more than 1 litre of petrol. At the same time it is planned that two pulp-paper mills, owned by Botnia and Ence, are going to use 86 million litres of water per day, taken from the Uruguay River.

Mi Guapo,

Remember the three pickled snakes in jars in the shop window of the pharmacy? A grass snake, an aspic adder, and an adder with a wider mouth. You told me about sucking the venom out of a friend's snake bite when you were a boy. When Idelmis comes into the shop each morning, the first thing she does is to check the snakes by touching each jar. Maybe she's not checking them but announcing her arrival to them. After all, it's her pharmacy. Then she puts on her white overall and kisses me.

Her pharmaceutical memory is still extraordinary. She knows precisely where each medicine is to be found and what its active ingredients are and the precautions they imply. When there are not too many people waiting, she tends to sit at a little table between the antispasmodics and ointments, where she reads a book. Nearly always a travel book. Her favourite word is still Discovery. She's hidden there so she can choose to ignore those who come in for advice or for a particular medicine. Only when somebody's complaint or question interests her, or when it's somebody she has known for fifty years, does she appear and take over.

Then she's impressive. She belongs to the generation of the first women pharmacists. A woman for whom science was a sister. And for her the pharmaceutical is close to the maternal. She adjusts her hair, looking into the mirror above the sink near the mouthwashes, and with her slow words and her nodding memories, she reassures all those who come in for reassurance.

Yet when she takes off her white overall and leaves the Sucrat pharmacy to walk home through the bus station, she's a frail, hesitant, old woman. She's aged since you've seen her. So have I. And if she goes on working, it's because she needs to feel close to cures. Sometimes I envy her.

The word recently has altered since they took you. Tonight I don't want to write how long ago that was. The word recently now covers all that time. Once it meant a few weeks or the day before yesterday. Recently I had a dream.

In the dream there was a road, a dangerous one, much ambushed. Deep ruts. Dusty. Without any cover. Many had lost their lives or been wounded there on different occasions – this I knew in my dream. It was somehow written on the broken surface of the road. I was walking down it, heartbroken but not frightened. Maybe it was the road of our refugees. I think this now because such things happen in dreams, but when I was in the dream I didn't think it. I simply walked. And at a certain moment, on my right, there was a high stony escarpment, high as the wall of a room. I stopped and with difficulty climbed up it to the top. And there what did I see? I don't know what words to use. The words are never there. But between the useless words you'll see what I saw. Several piles, dumps, loads, heaps, of plums, blue plums, covered with frost. And two things, my love, were surprising. First of all the size of the heaps – each heap could have filled a freight train of forty wagons. They weren't high but they were very wide and long. And the second thing was their colour. Despite the white frost, the blue of the plums was sunny and incandescent. Make no mistake about it, it wasn't the blue of any sky, it was the blue of small ripe plums. And their blue is what I send you in your cell tonight as I write in the dark.

A'ida

Price of gold over US$700 an ounce.

Habibi,

The first light of a new day has begun its irrevocable ascent. It begins decidedly; a decision has been taken. Neither by them with their helicopters, nor by us. Maybe one day more things will be clearer about who decides what.

The first light over there to the left, moistening the horizon in the east, is the colour of diluted milk, four parts water, one part skimmed milk.

There are times when I believe I have a few more months to live before dying after a long life; at other times I feel like an eleven year old, waiting to find out about almost everything.

Eight of us slept here, two children, three women, two men and myself. The children like me are already awake. They have fewer reasons than the adults for sleeping, fewer things they never want to see again.

There are times when I react immediately and instinctively like a mother, then I protect cunningly, heedless of any argument for or against.

At other times, mi Guapo, I'm ready to sacrifice what you call my manhood and to die fighting for that bitch of a justice who left long ago without a word!

Under my coat, folded up to make a pillow, my mobile beeped twice. Text message on screen more luminous than the sky: Our heads are never low enough to eat their shit.

Your
A'ida

P.S. Your letter about donkeys made me laugh a lot.

On my way to the pharmacy there was this man, whom I didn't recognise, sitting on the edge of the road by the roundabout, down the hill where the mulberry tree is. Beside him was a smashed bicycle with a buckled front wheel. He was about your age but nothing like you.

No other man is like you. Everything is made of the same stuff, and everyone is put together differently.

It wasn't clear whether he had fallen off his bicycle or whether it had been stolen and he had just found it. You could tell, though, by the way he touched it that it was his bike. One of his trouser legs was torn which suggested he might have fallen off. At the same time all his clothes were shabby and his sandals broken and down-at-heel. He could have fallen off, or his bike might have been pinched whilst he was asleep, and it was the thief who fell off.

When you're alone a lot like I am, you get to speculating about stupid things like this. If you had been with me I wouldn't have given it a thought. I didn't ask him about what had happened because he was obviously thinking hard about what to do next. His forearms on his knees, his chin on his hands, the toe of his left sandal seeking shelter beneath the instep of his right boot, nosing its way in. He was on the point of taking a decision. At such moments many of you men have this special look. It's as if you were willing yourselves to disappear, about to dissolve into the sky. A minuscule martyrdom. Women are different. They take most decisions sitting firmly on their arses.

I've just taken one. Why don't we get married? You ask me! I say yes! Then we ask them. If they give their permission, I visit you for the wedding, and once a week forever after in the visiting room!

Every night I put you together – bone by delicate bone.

Your A'ida

Bolivia. 12 million acres of land given to landless rural workers. Another 142 million hectares will be redistributed, if plan works out, to 2.5 million people. A quarter of the population. Tonight, Evo Morales, you are here with us. Come and sit in my cell that measures 2.5m x 3m.

Kanadim, my wing,

I've been seeing Soko a lot these days. Her nephew has disappeared without trace. Her sister-in-law is dying in hospital. Her husband's taxi has cracked up, so he's not earning, and Soko's sewing takes much longer now, and she can't take on more because her eyesight is failing, and she needs a cataract operation which she'll never be able to afford. Without money there's nothing, she says, nothing.

She laments every evening and God knows she has reason enough, and in her nightly lamentation all the misfortunes become equal so she can weave them together as strands in the same continuous prayer asking God to forgive and have mercy on her, Amen.

And this evening while she was lamenting, I thought: if only it was you listening to her! You would show her how to separate her complaints out, and then examine them, one by one, to decide what can be changed and what can't be changed.

Taking things apart, putting them together, I think of your father's radio. The photo of your father is where we put it on the second shelf of the bookcase. You both have the same high forehead. But his was more wind-beaten.

It was a special market day, there was no school. How old were you? Ten I think. I must ask your mother. Your father went with friends to look at cattle. And you, left on your own, took your father's radio to pieces, laying the pieces out one by one on the rug. Your mother complained and wrung her hands. When your father came back he kept shouting: Why? Why? How could you do this? Why? It was working, the radio! Why? So I can put it together again, you whispered, and your father lowered his arm. I'll give you two hours, just two hours, and by midnight he was handing you the last pieces as you asked for them, and next morning you listened to the news together, both of you.

The news next morning, you always insist, was about the murder in Paris of Ben Barka, just before the Havana Conference. There's something about the way you say this which makes me think of an emergency landing! Maybe the radio news was totally unmemorable next morning. The real news was that you could undo a radio and fit it together again!

With you, Soko would examine her misfortunes one by one. And between each she'd give a sad smile which would become progressively less sad.

I miss you now – your A'ida

"No, we do not want to catch up with anyone. What we want to do is to go forward all the time, night and day, in the company of Man, in the company of all men. The caravan should not be stretched out, for in that case each line will hardly see those who precede it; and men who no longer recognise each other, meet less and less together, and talk to each other less and less."

I learnt that warning by heart somewhere. I asked Durito who said he thought it was Fanon.

Mi Guapo, Mi Soplete, my Kanadim, Ya Nour,

The other day Andrea asked me how we first met – you and I. And I told her. Now I want to tell you. We can change it, if you like. The past is the one thing we are not prisoners of. We can do with the past exactly what we wish. What we can't do is to change its consequences. Let's make the past together. How many years ago was it? Anyway it was midsummer and very hot and you were repairing a lorry, an open lorry. There were other vehicles there – several of them without wheels, propped up on stones. In a hollow on a hillside west of Sennacherib. There was a flat-roofed concrete building with small windows, which must once have been a house for a family. You used it to keep your tools in. There were a couple of benches. Also a bed with a tattered rug beside it, so perhaps sometimes you slept there. Outside there was a linden tree which gave some shade.

I was meant to deliver a car battery. I remember carrying it. It was heavy and filthy. So when I got out of my car I held it with my fingers under its top flange so it wouldn't touch my sleeves.

Put it down, you shouted as soon as you saw me approaching.

You were welding something. You wore a leather apron and apart from that a pair of shorts. In front of your face was a dark metal shield.

When you emerged from behind it, you were wearing a black patch over your right eye, and your face was screwed up as if in pain.

Is your eye hurt? I asked.

It's inflamed, you replied, and I had to go to the hospital. It happens with this – and you held up the welder.

You were wearing heavy leather boots without socks and with their laces undone.

Where are you from? you asked me.

I told you and explained how a guy in the petrol station, seeing I was taking this road that nobody takes, had asked me to deliver the battery.

You looked me up and down and murmured, thank you.

How long do you have to keep the patch on your eye? I asked.

Until I find gold! you said.

Then, smiling, you slowly strode towards me and took it off.

Agree to this version?

A'ida.

Delocalisation. Refers not only to the practice of moving production and services to where labour is cheapest, but also to the plan of destroying the status of all earlier fixed places so that the entire world becomes a Nowhere, and a single liquid market.

Such a Nowhere has nothing to do with deserts. Deserts have stronger profiles than mountains. No desert forgives. Flying over Haserof so low – undercarriage retained – the tips of two blades of the propellor were buckled back. Discovered it only on landing at Faz. I was still learning.

This prison is not Nowhere.

It happens, when I'm not holding you between my legs, that I think of you as the hero in a story I once heard. Not a story I'm inventing, a story I once heard in a bus before they ordered us to get down. I couldn't invent you, if I lived a hundred lives.

In the story you're looking up at some graffiti you've painted high up on a blind wall near the airport, and you're smiling, you're proud of yourself – as if the words were a kite you had just launched! And because you're a kid, you're careless and you don't see them approaching. So you're still smiling, proud of yourself, when they frogmarch you into the half-track. Then they paint over the slogans, and an old woman says: They have painted everything white, as if nothing has happened, but the walls are still shouting underneath the coat of paint!

And in gaol, that first time, you meet Alexis. I saw him last week. He still has the same wart by his left nostril. (Salicyclic acid ($C_7H_6O_3$) would remove it, applied daily, but never on the skin around it.) He still stutters when excited. We played a hand or two together.

Friends made in prison are different from others, aren't they? They joke more. They bring an old joke out of their pocket, they take a bite and then they offer it around. And they arrive differently. Even if they've travelled hundreds of kilometres, they turn up unannounced and without any explanation. And they know with certainty that they are welcome.

They also have their own way of deciding when to refer to something serious. Always at an unexpected moment – getting into a car, the front seat tilted forward, or when clearing plates off a table at the end of a meal. And they are very scrupulous about signs. With their eyes they scribble a receipt for the smallest message received. They never look blank.

I'm looking into your eyes, and I am not your friend, I'm your woman. And I want to tell you something.

The ephemeral is not the opposite of the eternal. The opposite of the eternal is the forgotten. Some pretend that the forgotten and the eternal are, when it comes down to it, the same thing. And they're wrong.

Others say the eternal needs us, and they are right. The eternal needs you in your cell and me here writing to you and sending you pistachio nuts and chocolate.

Tell me about your foot. I need to know.

Your A'ida.

However good a law is, it is invariably clumsy. This is why its application should be disputed or questioned. And the practice of doing this corrects its clumsiness and serves justice.

There are bad laws which legalise injustice. Such laws are not clumsy, for they enforce, when applied, exactly what they were intended to enforce. And they have to be resisted, ignored, defied. But of course, compañeros, our defiance of them is clumsy!

Mi Soplete,

You can tell by looking at the loaf that it's still too hot to hold. Twenty men waiting in the bakery down the street from the pharmacy at 6 pm. They always let me go first if I'm wearing my white overall. They wait for as long as a quarter of an hour and watch the bread being taken out. It seems to me we never had time to do this. The baker doesn't glance at the men, he keeps his eyes on the bread and on the embers at the back of the white hot vault. And the men wait attentively as if watching some kind of contest. I want to tell you something else too.

There's such a difference between hope and expectation. At first I believed it was a question of duration, that hope was awaiting something further away. I was wrong. Expectation belongs to the body, whereas hope belongs to the soul. That's the difference. The two converse and excite or console each other but the dream of each one is different. I've learnt something more. The expectation of a body can last as long as any hope. Like mine expecting yours.

As soon as they gave you two life sentences, I stopped believing in their time.

A.

P.S. Did you get the radishes sent by courier?

The schoolmaster (whose thick glasses a herder broke) quoted this to us: "The loveliest things we no longer see are sunlight, clear stars on a dark night, the full moon, and summer fruit – ripe cucumbers, pears, apples." Written only yesterday, the schoolmaster said, only 2,500 years ago.

I'm sitting on the ledge of the roof, where we used to sit together when the evenings were stifling. I think you could walk blindfold across the roofs I'm looking over. You know them so well. Your evenings now, you say in the last letter, have become longer because, since one week, they return you alone to your cell three hours before closedown as a punishment for a speech you made.

When they informed you about this, I'm sure they could read nothing on your face. I love your secrecy. It's your candour. Two F16s have passed over flying low. Because they can't break our secrets, they try to break our eardrums. I love your secrecy. Let me tell you what I can see at this moment.

Crammed windowsills, clotheslines, TV satellite dishes, some chairs propped against a chimney stack, two bird cages, a dozen improvised tiny terraces with their innumerable pots for plants and their saucers for cats. If I stand up I can smell mint and molokhiyya. Cables, telephone and electric, looping in every conceivable direction and every month sagging more. Eduardo still carries his bicycle up three flights of stairs and padlocks it to a cable by his chimney. Neighbours have moved in whom you don't know. I'm sending you a couple to keep you company. When they've left, I'll come.

Ved goes to bed early for he gets up at two every morning

to go to work. It's his choice, he works alone, smelting scrap metal he has found in the streets. Fifty-nine years old. I know because I asked him one day. He looks younger. He's from Sada. His father was a fisherman.

And that explains my green eyes, he says. He arrived three years ago.

He says nothing about why he came here or his life before. It's too long a story to tell, he says.

You could tell a part of it.

It would make no sense.

You have children?

Five.

Where are they?

Three boys and two girls.

You saw them recently?

They are far away, I haven't seen them for years.

They write to you?

I don't read.

Somebody else could–

They wouldn't write to somebody else.

So they do write to you?

No, because they know I can't read.

You don't want news of them?

One of them telephones me each Sunday, they take it in turn, so I speak to each one every five weeks. They bought me a cell phone.

Where did you say they were?

Far away and here – he lays a hand on his heart. They're all in different places and they all meet here. He moves the fingers of the hand placed against his heart.

I didn't ask him about his wife because I could see on his hand two wedding rings; he's a widower.

Strange what inspires trust. I know little about Ved and he's evasive, yet I'd trust him totally, and it's a physical quality, something to do with the way his body hears what he's saying, as if he finds something in his body before pulling it into words.

Once I was coming back late – after an evening of cards – we made 4 black canastas that evening – and there was Ved already leaving his apartment to go to work. I stop and we exchange greetings. Meanwhile I spot a fox down the street, waiting on the corner. I point silently towards the corner and smile. Ved takes note and turns very slowly in that direction. Then he folds his arms. He's waiting for me, he says, often we walk together to the ramparts before going our separate ways, I to my workshop and he to the garbage dumps. At night there's another life. I've seen the lights on in your pharmacy when you're working late, we don't talk about it but we notice, there's another life, very different. Very different, and those who work at night become deeply attached to the night and to others working in it. Time is much kinder at night, there's nothing to wait for, nothing is out of date at night.

He turns to look at the corner, smiles and makes a little bow towards me.

Sleep well, you who visit the sick at all hours, Signora A'ida, sleep well.

You'll know he's Ved, mi Guapo, because he's very tall. 2 metres tall. And he walks with a limp. You can talk about nights with him.

Now your second visitor. She's at her window, shedding beans. Six metres away. We often chat. Tonight she can see I'm writing. Everyone knows that when I'm writing on my knee, I'm writing to you. A few hours ago Ama was praying. She doesn't pray regularly every day. She prays fervently after she has split on someone, thus hoping to insure that she's still on good terms with everyone! Naive? Not really. She lives for the moment and forces whoever happens to be with her to do the same. Like sharing a last crust. She sells stolen cigarettes to people waiting at the bus station. Her room is barely larger than your cell. For water she has to go down to the yard. Climbing the stairs she carries a pitcher on her head – like she did when she posed for a postcard and got paid.

She smiles at everybody not with her eyes but with her mouth. And with her shoulders she keeps men at bay.

When we chat between our two windows or climb out on to the roof to watch the sun go down, she stops smiling and her mouth goes sad and she seeks my hand to hold it.

She will tell you the story of her death. She was found almost drowned in the sea. I had the feeling of being slowly sipped up, she says, of being drunk! I was gliding down the drinker's gullet and it was agreeable, rewarding, very agreeable, because I knew I tasted sweet!

Ama's nineteen.

When I hold a letter of yours in my hand, what I feel first is your warmth. The same warmth that's in your voice when you sing. I want to press myself against it but I don't, for, if I wait, the warmth will surround me on every side. Then when I reread the letter and I'm surrounded by your warmth, the words you've written belong to the distant past and we are looking back at those words together. We are in the future. Not the one we know so little about. We are in a future which has already begun. We are in a future that has our name. Hold my hand. I kiss the scars on your wrist.

Your A'ida.

They can't foresee what we intend to do next. This is why they lose their nerve. They can't cross the zone of silence they herd us into. A zone bordered on their side by the distant din of their false accusations, and on our side by our silent final intentions.

Ya Nour,

He was once a barber, a good listener. Gassan lives in the Wind's Arsehole neighbourhood. He has a small house he built himself when young, thirty years ago. Working at weekends and in the long summer evenings, it took him five years. Around it are several other houses today fallen into ruin. It's bitingly cold there in the winter but that hasn't changed for centuries. Last year Gassan lost his wife. All he has now is his passion for growing flowers.

He came into the pharmacy last week. He has that careful way of walking which old men – but seldom old women – sometimes develop. As if they are carrying a full basin of water they don't want to spill over. Come to think of it, it may be connected with prostate troubles. He came with a prescription for hytrine which is a terazosine. After I explained the dosage, he invited me to come and see his flowers one day. And this morning I was passing nearby so I strolled over. He showed me his irises. Copper-coloured ones, with writing in black on the inside of the petals. Always the same phrase. I lowered my eyes in admiration and he offered me one. Then he recited something like this: My wife, who is about to leave, is indoors talking with the gods, and already Separation, like a bad monkey, is swinging across the window . . .

I didn't reply, for he himself was replying to something he'd observed. He was comparing his sense of loss and mine. And me, I was comparing his lived-in house with the houses in ruins around it. They'd all been more or less the same size, two rooms, one floor, thirteen corners, a thousand and one secrets. Now the ruins look smaller. In his house the radio was on – a woman singer. Cesaria Evora. The ruined houses, by contrast, were silent. It was as if the sound of Evora's voice meticulously skirted around them.

He invited me in for coffee, turned off the radio. There are moments, he said as he sipped his coffee, when she is not dead. They multiply as the day goes on. But each day begins with her absence.

For me this isn't true; the day doesn't begin with your absence. It begins with the decision we took together to do what we are doing.

I remember the first time I watched you examining a machine that wasn't performing and looking for a way to fix it. It was a printer attached to a computer. You remember what we needed to print? It was so long ago.

You were wearing a white shirt with wide sleeves which you had rolled up to your armpits. We were in a basement behind the market in Abades. Your arm-hairs were very curly, each one like a figure 8. You had taken the casing off the printer and were studying the connectique.

On the Abades main street they were making a raid with two humvees. Methodically, centimetre by centimetre, you proceeded from point to point of the connectique. In your left hand an electric screwdriver, small as a wren with several beaks. Occasionally you tapped with it. I could see – for it was visible in your shoulders – that you were not only following wires, you were tracing the thinking process by which men had conceived and then constructed that machine.

In the main street shots were being fired.

Let's try this, you whispered. And I suddenly took in that with manmade machines there are circuits of ingenuity which can be shared between minds. Like poetry is shared. I saw this in the backs of your hands.

No words have ever been as reassuring to me as your hands were at that moment. We could hear their orders being shouted through a loud hailer in the main street. You looked up, directly at me, you nodded. And then winked with one of your sore eyes.

A.

The Inuit poet, Panegoosho, dropped in and started to talk about people she knew as a child. "They did not even try to be beautiful, only true, but beauty was there, it was a custom."

Ya Nour,

On the other side of the world, last Wednesday, they came as the day was ending. At that moment when people are saying to themselves – after the day's work . . . now it's over, no rush, take it easy . . .

They came to search, interrogate and scare. Too many of them for us to count. Each one with gun and grenades. I felt old, I could still remember the time when soldiers were warriors, when mothers, however anxious, were proud of their soldier sons.

Over there! You dirt monkeys! Move over! Quicker than that. Shit. What ya waiting for?

As I obeyed and watched I felt very close to you. They divided us into groups: men and women, elderly (not so dangerous) and dangerous. I was still amongst the dangerous, I'm glad to say. Each group was driven into a separate corner. Some of the elderly asked if they might sit. When you've answered, not a moment before.

Across the world, uniformed, highly armed, commanded soldiers operate against captured unarmed civilians, temporarily isolated and surrounded. This is the new military profession. Of course it has awlways happened. But before it wasn't systematic.

Soldiers have been transformed into bastards. And the old woman – your old woman – remembers Aeschylus.

They sent forth men to battle,
But no such men return;
And home, to claim their welcome,
come ashes in an urn . . .
They praise him through their tears and say
'He was a soldier,' or 'He died
nobly, with death on every side!'

The old military orders of Advance or Withdraw or Offer Covering Fire have become obsolete because there is no front line and no opposing army.

Nobody will say of one of these bastards that he died nobly.

If one of them happens to get killed, those close to him will mourn his death, but about its circumstances they will keep quiet, and say nothing.

The single word that counted on Wednesday was the one that came from the muzzle of a gun, addressed to somebody on their knees.

Better to choose our hour than to accept this.

We know each other. We've known each other from the time of Crocodilopolis.

[Letter unsent]

Mi Guapo,
Immense Manda, the music teacher arrived here last Wednesday. She turned up without a word of warning. There she was beaming as she advanced across the pharmacy, flapping her arms at the very last moment like a quail taking to the air.

When our friendship began she rescued me from the despair of the first-time prisoner – I was not yet eighteen. I've told you the story. Having just re-seen her, I want to tell it again. Every kind of love adores repetitions because they defy time. As you and I do.

In Lamasgao we had six hours compulsory work sewing uniforms, and on my first morning Manda chose to take the empty place beside me. I saw her approaching like a crowded bus that had crossed the Sierra; all the passengers, who knew each other after the long journey, were joking inside her.

You look as though you want things to get worse! This was the first thing she said to me. I nodded. They're getting worse, she said, one more push, I know it's hard but you can do it, one more push and you'll be at shit bottom. There! You've made it.

When Manda smiles it's like a rain that runs down the deep lines of her face, and at that moment she smiled, keeping her hand holding the big needle high in the air, whilst the smile drenched her face.

When's your birthday? she asked me next morning whilst sewing on an epaulette. And I told her because I wanted to climb into her bus. There was a place for me.

She hasn't changed much. Her shock of black hair is dyed black and she still shakes it in the same way. Her dark eyes still alter their size dramatically, according to what she's hearing. What's new is that she has learnt to play the lute.

I'm not certain of the details. She pretends that playing a lute can give her an entry to somewhere she wants to be. Some institution. Some committee. Maybe some building. So she took lessons.

The lute is like no other instrument, she says. As soon as you hug a lute, it becomes a man! You're playing a man. You feel it immediately. You pluck the strings – seven, thirteen or twenty-one according to your taste – you pluck the strings of his chest, of his neck, of his shoulders. A lute's music is male, male. You remember all the men you've ever played.

With her thick arms she imitates the gestures of playing a trombone, of making a trumpet call, of hiding a mouth-organ against the mouth, of wheedling a cello. There's a kind of turtle without a shell, she goes on, who's called a lute, because he's beautiful and has the same shape as the musical instrument! But who wants to play turtles, when you can play a man?

With a lute on your knees, you play the first tune in the world – suddenly she stops and we go on laughing and laughing 'til the laugh stops.

Then she turns to me, her eyes very small, and whispers:

in six months you and Xavier will be together, don't ask me where, don't ask me how, you'll be together is all I know.

She stayed three nights – I slept on the divan – and she left for Mirar this morning. Last night I invited some friends and cooked and she told stories and started talking about names, peoples names.

In the beginning, she said, there were two names, no more, a name for women and a name for men. Quickly from each of the two shot out others which were variants, versions, of the first one. As time went by, the names given to people across the entire world, became more ingenious and more various, until most of them no longer recognised one another. Yet, unlike other words, people's names, however strange-sounding and unfamiliar, possess, whenever we hear or pronounce them, a common sound. It's not in the syllables, it's not A'ida. It's not Karim. It's not Shasno. It's not Ybarra. The sound is something that surrounds the names.

Manda shut her eyes and went on talking. The sound comes, I believe, from their velocity. Velocity is like a name, isn't she? All the world's names are rushing at the speed of light to converge on their point of origin, or else they are advancing at the speed of light to disintegrate into particles smaller than electromagnetic photons . . . I'm not sure which, but it doesn't matter. All that matters is that names are not like other words. That's why I'm learning the lute.

Ah! The music teacher!

From my name to your name!

From A'ida to Xavier

"After almost 200 years we can say that the USA was designed to fill the entire world with poverty – whilst giving it the name of Freedom. The United States empire is the greatest threat which exists in the world today . . ."

Chavez, Moscow 27/07/2006

Mi Soplete,

Through the window far away on the other side of Dimitri's house I can see a dog walking slowly and sniffing the earth. Like me, he is looking for something and doesn't know what. Let's say he is looking intently, all his senses alert, for a surprise. And I'm looking for words to tell you how I'm with you.

One of the funny things a woman can offer a man is a curved roof. Don't laugh. Pagodas are feminine.

As soon as a woman is living in a room, its ceiling curves. You haven't noticed? If she's wretched in the room, it droops like a torn sleeve. If she's OK it rolls on and on like the hills of Galilee. To have the effect, it's not enough for a woman to visit a room, she has to live in it. It's a phenomenon like weather, it has to go on for months.

If it goes on for months, it's as if cyclones and anti-cyclones cross the ceiling and make it billow, and as if Geometry has gone out to play backgammon and never came back. No more right angles. Only slopes.

A man lies down on the floor of such a room, and the ceiling, instead of being above him, comes beside him, fits his body. Lie on your bunk. I'm sending you a curved roof.

I drive to Mirar, where we used to go and eat on your birthday. I take the same path as we took.

The sun is low in the sky. The sun is short-sighted. It doesn't spot what changes. The folds of land falling from the mountain stay the same. The sun knows them. (It's very dry; it hasn't rained for two months.) As soon as the slopes level out a bit, the dwellings and the shacks start. And here there are small changes every hour, which the sun doesn't notice.

The chozas are sitting side by side, their doors open, talking about the hassles of the day, the latest deaths, who has become pregnant and where to fetch water tonight. A thousand homes. Each with its sudden secrets.

They have put you where you are to separate you from these secrets. So I'm sending them to you, as the sun goes down. They can't read them, you can and so can –

your
A'ida

P.S. Look at the ceiling.

The enemy cannot be attacked directly. Approached frontally the enemy is impregnable. Approached frontally the enemy has to be recognised as victor. To continue as victor the enemy needs new frontal enemies. They do not exist; so the enemy invents them. We await this as our opportunity for countless side attacks. This is the strategy of resistance.

The other night I was crossing the Wind's Arsehole neighbourhood at 2 am. I was going to give an injection (tranexamic acid 2.5gr.) to a woman who had had a miscarriage and was losing too much blood (the Furik road to the hospital was blocked). The foetus was four months old, a boy, and the mother, Miriam, was as devastated as a bombarded town.

On my way back I passed Ved who was collecting metal in his cart. He started talking about techniques for extracting honey from honeycombs. The flowers are finished and it is time to collect from the hives, this must be why he launched into the subject. No method is perfect, he said, but perfection is always unlovable. What we love are blemishes.

Then he looked up at the night sky and I studied his worn face in the ensuing silence. He's the age my father would have been. Blemishes! he repeated.

As I drove off I thought of the scars above your right wrist. Burn scars. Blemishes. They were the first distinguishing mark I noticed about you. Strange term Distinguishing Mark, isn't it? Coined for their police records and stripping procedures.

Eyes have only four or five official adjectives: brown, blue, hazel, green! The colour of your eyes is Xavier

In your last letter you say Jaimes is running a course on mathematics which twelve of you are attending. Wait a moment for I want to find a quotation which I think is in a notebook I kept when I was studying pharmaceutics in Tarsa.

It has taken me two hours to find it, but here it is, from nearly two thousand years ago.

There are properties common to all things, and the knowledge of this opens the mind to the greatest wonders of nature. The principal one includes the two infinities which are to be found in all things, infinite largeness and infinite smallness . . . Since nature has engraved her own image on all things and that of her author on all things, they almost all share her double infinity.

I see the scars on your wrist. I'm thinking of the years that pass. Of all my faults and blemishes, which one do you love particularly? Tell me, tell me slowly and quietly so we can enjoy it together during the long night!

Your
A'ida.

Cassandra Wilson on radio:

"I just want to see you
when the sun goes down.
It's as simple as that
I want to see you when the sun goes down
no more than that."

Mi Guapo,

Went to see your mother. All things considered, she's not bad. When you go through the front door you still have the feeling of kissing her straight on the mouth.

The kitchen spotless, shutters closed in the bedroom to keep it cool. She asked me to read out loud a letter she had from your brother in Covas. When I was young, she said, it wasn't so serious that I couldn't read or write, because people discussed everything that mattered, but today so much happens in silence, and you need to be able to read in order to know what people are deciding.

I read the letter out loud to her. Apparently he's making friends and money in Covas. If he wasn't, he would probably have said the same thing. After a certain age men often treat their mothers as if they were small children and they are wrong. Mothers, literate and illiterate, can take everything.

We drank green tea and talked about you.

Has he lost much weight?

I haven't seen him, Mother.

He's all right. I would know if he wasn't, she says.

She goes into the bedroom. I can hear her breathing heavily. When she comes back into the kitchen she is holding something wrapped in a tissue paper, the colour of cyclamen. She hands it to me to unwrap. I do so slowly. It's a ring with a blue lazurite stone. Lazurites belong to the silicate group. If you like, mi guapo, I can tell you their formula! $(Na,Ca)_8(AlSiO_4)_6(SO_4,S,Cl)_2$.

Do the precious stones of old women sparkle more than the jewels of other women? Perhaps. The jewels they wore when young retain the glow they themselves once had. Like the glow we see in certain flowers, immediately after the sun has gone down.

In the kitchen, your mother's deep blue lazurite glows on the palm of my hand.

You keep it for me, I say.

Xavier would like me to give it to you today, she announces.

They deferred our right to get married, I remind her.

Picking up the ring, she slips it over the fourth finger of my left hand. I make a gesture as if stroking a dog's head.

And your mother holds her breath, remembering in the immense stillness of her body how she made the same gesture with the same ring on her hand fifty years ago.

A.

To tell the truth? Words tortured until they give themselves up to their polar opposites; Democracy, Freedom, Progress, when returned to their cells, are incoherent. And then there are other words, Imperialism, Capitalism, Slavery, which are refused entry, are turned back at every frontier point, and their confiscated papers given to impostors such as Globalisation, Free Market, Natural Order.

Solution: the evening language of the poor. With this some truths can be told and held.

My on-the-ground-lion

We both know that the receiving and sending of mail is forbidden for those in solitary confinement and this doesn't stop me writing.

You'll read this letter some day, and when they next put you into the hole, I want you to remember what I say, so you can retell the story to yourself in the $2m^2$ where they bang us up to try to reduce us to shit.

I was twenty-four years old, we were both in Faz, it was Spring. We had first met nine months before.

I woke up early and you whispered to me – I remember we slept that night in a room on a ground floor with a passiflore bush outside the window – you whispered to me, let's go for a walk. And you added – wear jeans! I was about to argue, and I didn't for I sensed you had some plan. Your smile told me that.

We made coffee and drank it slowly. Then we walked towards the north of the town along a busy street with many villagers coming to market in their carts and vans. On the outskirts there was a school, and it must have been the moment for the midmorning break, for there were hundreds of kids milling around in the playground. Suddenly a ball, kicked wildly into the air, came across the street towards us and you ran a few steps to catch it! We grinned at one another. We heard a band of boys whistling and one of them was waving. You bounced the ball on the road several times and, with a lifting kick which propelled it way above the heads of the traffic, you sent it back to them! They cheered and waved again. And, instead of going on with their game, they kicked the ball, well-aimed this time, back to you. You caught it nimbly like before, and, laughing you threw it to me. More cheers. Shouts of Goalie! Goalie!

I ran across the street, the ball between my arms, and when I reached the grass verge on the other side, where there were two tethered goats grazing, I waited, facing the boys, to see what would happen. More cheers. Two boys pushed another who ran towards me, fell deliberately to his knees – much laughter – and held up his hands for the ball. The ball was blue and white and pretty tattered.

When I came back, you took hold of my two hands and clapped them together.

We walked another kilometre and came to an airfield. Two hangars. Three propellor planes on the grass. A tarmac runway the length of two soccer fields. It was then I caught on – we were going to fly!

I'm giving you my version. Yours won't be the same. You were the pilot. For me everything was for the first time – like on a honeymoon.

We went into an office and you talked to a friend. We drank tea. Years ago the two of you had flown together. Sometimes I miss it, you said to him.

Then you turned to me and said: Take everything out of your pockets, we want nothing to drop. I handed you my comb, my keys and the dice we used to play with when we had to wait interminably in some place.

When they next confiscate everything from you, before banging you up in the pit, tell yourself, my on-the-ground-lion, the story of how we flew in the CAP 10B. Listen to my voice telling it. Our two versions will be one then.

You strapped a parachute to my back. Arranging the length of the straps of a parachute for your beloved, winding them and crossing them and fixing the clasps shut, is, strangely, not so different from unbuttoning or unzipping whatever the beloved is wearing and slipping off the clothes. It requires a similar attention before the stark facts.

Not too tight around the heart, you said, for the heart needs to move, but firmly between the legs. I caught on about the wearing of trousers.

Nothing easier in the world than to open it, but wait till you're clear of the aircraft!

The word aircraft made me smile for it sounded like a flying instructor's word and suddenly – as I hadn't done before – I pictured you as a young pupil!

Pull with your right hand the ring in front of your left shoulder, pull it across your body and the parachute will open, we're not going to need it, but it's stupid to have one on your back and not know how it operates.

The word operates was like the word aircraft. I saw you studiously taking notes. Don't worry, I joked, I'll wait for you!

You put on your parachute, and you and I walked across the grass to a hangar. Inside was the CAP 10B. Push her out, you said and we pushed. I was expecting a small plane but I had no idea how light it was. An Apache weighs several tons. A CAP, I reckoned, weighed only about thirty-five times as much as the two parachutes we were carrying on our backs. This astounding lightness and the glimpse of you as you must have been when you were a pupil made me feel suddenly frivolous. Nothing else mattered.

Step up on to the wing, angel, not on the elevator flap, on the wing here with both feet, hold on to the handle at the top of the windscreen and lower yourself into the cockpit, arse well back in the seat, no sitting on the edge. I'll join you in a minute. You went to check the gas with a dipstick. Then you disappeared under the nose and I supposed you were examining the wheels of the undercarriage. You strolled to the tip of each wing and moved the flaps up and down so that the two broomsticks in the cockpit leaned left, right, left, right.

You did everything very slowly, and watching you, I thought of a horseman lifting each leg of his horse to examine its hooves before mounting and beginning a long journey. You know me though, I'm hopeless, I'm from deep in the forest! And suddenly you surprised me – for you patted the fuselage of the CAP and scratched it, digging your nails in, as if it had a coat!

You climbed in beside me and fastened our harnesses. You explained how it was a double-control plane for instructing pilots. The pupil's always on the left, you said. Which is where I was. The cockpit, my love, of the CAP is smaller than the hole.

You plugged in the headphones, tested the radio. I listened to your voice. It came no longer from you sitting there beside me; I heard it in my head. Say something, you asked, just checking, say something! I didn't know you could kick a ball so well! It was luck, you said in my head.

You reached up and slid the glass roofing forwards, and over us. It clicked shut. How many abductions on horseback have been sung about? None was like this one of ours. You explained the clocks to me. Revs per minute. Km per hour. Altimeter. Turn and Bank Level Indicators. Compass.

Nobody in front? It was a ritual question. A man on the grass with headphones made a thumbs-up sign. You checked the rudder bar with both feet, like a goose waddling, and you started the motor.

The engine noise filled the cockpit and it was similar to the noise of the sea except that it vibrated.

I was clinging to you hard, not with my arms, because it was not your body I was clinging to, we were both sitting well back in our seats, very calm, I was clinging to your intentions, your exact intentions. What they were I couldn't tell because I knew nothing about flying, but the way you intended whatever it was, was deeply familiar to me, and inseparable from my love for you.

We taxied to the end of the runway. 1,200 rpm 2,000 rpm You took your left hand off the stick and touched my right knee, you returned your hand to the stick, pushed the throttle forward with your right hand, your sleeve edged up, and I could see the scars, and the runway began to slip towards and under us, quite slowly and then gathering its own speed.

I didn't feel us leaving the ground. You did. At a given moment the runway relaxed and we were no longer touching. We were flying two metres or five metres above the earth, I couldn't judge our height. I only registered our freedom, and the ailerons, as you taught me to call the flaps, were still out.

The airfield was way behind before you coaxed the stick a little back, pushed the gas full open, and the CAP soared, leaving everything below.

It's not a sensation of being either lifted or being drawn up, is it? It's a sensation of growing, of growth. When someone is remembered and emerges from oblivion, maybe they feel like we did. After a minute we levelled out.

You take over now, you told me, aim for the cumulus that looks like a cat, yes, that one, aim for its back and keep the same altitude. We are at 1,500 feet.

I glanced down to my left. The houses, wagon tracks, village streets, dunes, trees were still distinct. If I'd known their names, I could have named each one. I thought about napalm and the height from which they choose to spray.

A little to your right, your voice said in my head, and I moved the stick and we banked more steeply than I expected. You forgot your right foot, you said in my head, laughing.

I don't want to learn, I want to be flown – like a President!

OK, you said, and we climbed another 500 ft. Out of range of persuasion, on our own.

We'll do a slow roll, you said in my head, we won't change direction, we'll maintain the same altitude and we'll turn 360 degrees, like a screw. Ready?

I nodded. We flew on as before. You were waiting. I love the way you wait, I love the way you choose moments. High above us a jet flew over – flying east and leaving its white trail, which was semitransparent against the blue, and different from the white of the cumulus clouds which looked so permanent.

Tell me if I'm wrong, but it seems to me that after this flight of ours above Faz, you never had the chance to pilot again? The recent years I know about, but even before? It was your last flight and my first.

When the moment arrived, you decided. I was watching you. You moved the broomstick a little forward and very firmly to the left. Almost, but not quite immediately – the time to lick my lips – we banked more and more steeply till my wing was pointing up like a mast. After that I could make nothing out. Earth and sky furled and unfurled like a flag from the mast, and time vanished. When level stops existing, time stops too doesn't it?

We were turning together – this is all I knew. Capsuled and turning together.

How long did our roll last – seconds, a minute, a lifetime? I didn't know.

The nose of the CAP was again parallel to the horizon and three fingers' width below it. The three fingers' width, you told me, shows we're flying more or less level. I looked at you, you were smiling. I put my hand on your knee. We flew on. Nothing except the sound of the motor. The little motor with only the power of a big motorbike.

Another? your voice in my head asked. Why not? I said.

You banked this time left and my wing went down and down. Less taken by surprise than before, I could feel the inside of my body, I felt its organs turning and jostling. These organs weren't what they look like in an anatomy book, each one with its neat shape and its definite name – liver, heart, uterus, suprarenal gland, bladder – no, they were unravelling, intermingling, fingering each other! And they were all me!

During the roll this time, scale vanished. The performing organs in my body, sitting beside you, became the same size as the forests, the hillsides, the delta I saw below to my right.

You, concentrating on where we were going, were looking exactly ahead. Straight. You were also piloting inside my body, mi Soplete. And it only happened to us once! Only once. Days later you told me I cried out. What kind of cry? Like a bird in flight, you said, like a pipit.

We levelled out again. Motor regular. Nose three fingers' width below the horizon. When the wind varied, the CAP feathered. Sun to the right.

Fernando's with us, you announced, it was Fernando who taught me to fly a ULM nine years ago. They killed him last year. He's with us now. What I admired about Fernando was his capacity to persuade people to be honest with themselves, for when this happens they gain the advantage of surprise. An incomparable tactical advantage in any insurrection. It's the lies we tell ourselves that make us repetitive. Fernando understood this.

2,500 rpm.

We do a loop?

I nodded.

At the top, I'm going to cut the motor, don't worry, it's so we can hear the silence.

So we did a loop, and later we did two more.

Your right hand went forward for maximum gas. You brought the stick defiantly towards you. We climbed steeply, and I knew you were going to make it a vertical climb. There was no ground visible anywhere, the ground was behind us.

We were pressed back against our parachutes with a weight that was so crushing it felt like fate and your job was to keep that weight there for as long as you could. Then the sound of the motor changed, the waves shifting the shingle sounded weaker and weaker.

I looked up and back, and there, behind my ears, I found the horizon.

It was coming over our two heads like the hem of a cape, being pulled over us. Smoothly, regularly, till it settled before our eyes, three fingers' width below the CAP's nose.

Time had already stopped for me but not for you – you were counting and observing and you had already cut the motor. In the ensuing silence the earth was above us and the sky below.

The two of us now weighed less than nothing. My body, weightless, no longer ended at my skin, it extended through the silence to the far side of everything I saw.

The silence was packed with distance, like my body, and, whilst you were calculating and following in the sky below the invisible trace of the circle we were making, this distance became intimate and close.

It cradled me as the CAP dived, gathering speed, motor turning, down, down towards the earth, which we could see like a curtain pulled across the entire windscreen.

You told me years later when we were sleeping every

night in a different room to avoid being found, that in the loops the instant of temptation is during the fourth and final 90-degree realignment, when one chooses life again and levels out.

Yet that choice, mi Soplete, was already there, was already prophesied in the distance and intimacy of the silence you piloted us through!

Three loops and with each one we brought back a little bit more of the limitless.

In the $2m^2$ of the pit I tell you this.

Last Thursday Andreas asked me whether I could look after Lily in the early part of the evening. She had to have her papers stamped at the Commissariat. Lily's four, you've never seen her except in a photo. She has a shock of curly hair, and when she's doing nothing else, she smiles. She and I get on well, even though we both know that she prefers men.

I walked with her through the market, for on the slope going down to the river a travelling fairground had been set up for the weekend. Dodgem cars, roundabouts, a bowling alley, stilts, skittles, swings. She spotted almost immediately what she wanted: a ride on the swings on chains that go round in a circle. The faster the machine turns the higher the swings go. She didn't want to ride alone, she wanted me to come with her.

I sat on the wooden seat and fixed the clasps of the strap that would hold me to the swing and then I did the same for Lily who sat on my lap. The music started and we began to turn very slowly. On all the other swings were kids, I was the only adult.

The one who screams loudest, announced the operator as he took up his position by the controls in the center of the roundabout, gets a free ride next time!

As we gathered speed, we swung out on the chains and we used our legs as pivots for continually changing the direction we were facing. The music went faster. We went faster with it. Round and round and round. Lily screamed like a bird in flight.

When finally the machine slowed down and I put my feet on the ground and unclasped our straps, the operator told Lily she could have a free ride. She hugged herself and said: This time by myself!

I did up her strap and walked to the side. When the swings were soaring at their highest and the music was at its loudest and Lily was screaming, I decided to write you this letter, my pilot, about the CAP 10B.

Your A'ida.

From welder to welder.

One million workers of the Third World. Dismantle for scrap the great aircraft carriers and passenger liners of the First World. The ship once grounded, with the wood and insulating material taken out, they cut into the hull with acetylene. Wherever there are traces of oil or petrol the flame risks to provoke an explosion. They wear no or little protective clothing. 20 to 30 accidents a day on the beach at Tossa. Welder's daily wage – 1 dollar.

I awoke at 3 am. On whatever it fell, the light was like grey ash. I got up, dressed and, without asking myself why, walked out into the street. The street lamps were off. I went walking towards the pharmacy out of habit. At one point I saw a fox and I thought of Ved. The nights are kinder, he said. Not this one, I said to myself, this one sees everything as trash.

I started walking faster and hearing the sound of my own footsteps and the silence waiting to cover them. And I thought: a woman can feel sorry for a man, she can console him, yet the consolation doesn't last long. I thought about men and how they like to greet one another as victors – even if their small victories have to be invented. The mutual acclaim they offer one another lasts no longer though than our brief consolation.

Then I heard the noise of a train approaching and I was scared because there's no railway. Truck after truck. I shut my eyes. A freight train not a passenger one, with many of us clinging to the roofs of the wagons.

With my eyes shut I thought: what lasts is women recognising the men they come to love as victors whatever happens, and men honouring each other because of their shared experience of defeat. This is what lasts!

The train that was passing, whistled, and the whistle reminded me of my grandfather in Tora. He earnt his living cleaning out passenger trains at night and he referred to their sidings as dormitories. The engines sleep there! he told me when I was five years old.

Your A'ida

Mi Soplete,

In the northeast corner of the quadrant, where the dumped tyres are, there's a rose bush. Near the eucalyptus tree. The rose bush has put out a shoot five metres long, and it creeps up the tree's trunk looking for light to flower into. Five metres! One hundred and thirty thorns! I counted them. To count I had to lift the tendril from time to time. And a couple of thorns pricked my arm. I don't know why I wanted to count them. Probably because I wanted to tell you about the determination of the rose. One hundred and thirty thorns.

You and I are between two generations. The first is made up of the company of those close to us, who died or were killed. Many of them younger than we have become. They are awaiting us with open arms.

The second is the company of the young, for whom we are an example. What we have chosen to live encourages them. With open arms they instruct us to go ahead . . .

We are between the two. If only, mi Guapo, we were in each other's arms!

Is it something I did a long time ago? Or is it something I wanted to do and haven't yet done? Anyway, I wanted to put my hand on a letter and draw its outline to send you. Sometime after – whenever it was – I came across a book which explained how to draw hands and I opened it, turning page after page. And I decided to buy it. It was like the story of our life. All stories are also the stories of hands – picking up, balancing, pointing, joining, kneading, threading, caressing, abandoned in sleep, cutting, eating, wiping, playing music, scratching, grasping, peeling, clenching, pulling a trigger, folding. On each page of the book there are careful drawings of hands performing a different action. So I'm going to copy one.

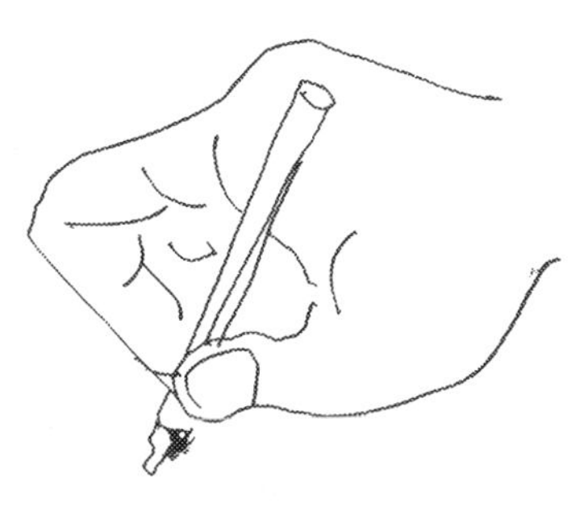

I'm writing to you.

Now I look down at my hands that want to touch you and they seem obsolete because they haven't touched you for so long.

Your A'ida

IMF WB GATT WTO NAFTA FTAA – their acronyms gag language, as their actions stifle the world.

Ya Nour,

I keep on asking: is your thumb better? Why don't you tell me?

In China there's a tree called Ginkgo Biloba. As trees go, it's a primitive species. The Chinese call it The Tree of a Hundred Shields. I want you to have every one of the hundred. Medicinally it stimulates blood circulation – specially for the legs. Ginkgo Biloba. I hear you pronouncing it. Using your deep voice.

You wrote to me – your last letter came a week ago – about how they shaved a woman prisoner. I know what she felt. It's like being chained hand and foot – till you learn to slip out of the chains. It takes about a week. But the hatred felt for the hands that did it is timeless.

It's three in the morning and perhaps you're not sleeping either.

One of the chairs was broken, its legs splayed, its seat was loose, the lateral struts between its legs wouldn't stay in their holes.

Eduardo was sitting on it, holding forth about how to teach literacy and suddenly it collapsed and there was Eduardo on his back on the floor! Laughing we picked up the pieces and put them in the corner.

And this morning, since I wasn't working, I decided to mend it. I'd already bought a pot of glue. Sticky and white like the juice in the stems of dandelions. I turned the broken chair upside down and sat on one of the others. I had a hammer, a screwdriver and a rag. The rag was the sleeve, or part of the sleeve, of a padded coat which Olga used to wear. It was clear what I had to do. I took every length of wood I could out of its hole. I reckoned that those that wouldn't budge were strong enough. Then I squeezed glue into all the empty holes and on to the tips of the legs and struts. I lined them up, eased each tip into its hole, and hammered the lengths home with the rag wrapped round the stained wood to protect it from the blows of the hammer. Everything was engaged and perfectly in place. I stood the chair on its legs and looked at it. And then a strange thing happened. I began to cry. I cried so much I couldn't see anything.

After I don't know how long, I went to wash the glue off my fingers and to clean my face.

When I came back there was the chair standing upright, everything together, and the excess glue around the holes waiting to be wiped off with the sleeve of Olga's coat. I wiped it off, tightened three screws and placed the chair by the window (the one through which we used to watch the cats on the roof). Wait two days for the glue to dry, I told myself.

What made me cry? Was it that the chair was so easy to mend and the rest is so hard? Or was it realising that I no longer depended on you for such tasks? On you!

It's the small things which frighten us. The immense things, which can kill, make us brave.

Your
A'ida

Tonight I was in the Junction district and I was passing a café I frequented when I was very young. On the spur of the moment I went in. Inside there was music. An accordion. Not being played in the café, but in a cellar below, to which there was a staircase.

The accordionist standing, head almost touching the beams, a few people sitting at tables and in the centre, a couple about to dance – or, perhaps, to dance again for a third or fifth time. She couldn't have been more than seventeen.

She stepped out alone, holding her arms a little apart from her body, waiting. Not for her partner who was watching her, bemused. Not for the accordionist who had begun playing. Not for another couple to join her. She was waiting to be carried away by the forces inside her. She was waiting for those forces to emerge. Calmly, her heels a little off the ground, her face open, wrists turned with their palms up, as if to see whether it was yet raining. When she felt the first drop, she would move.

The drops came! She circled twice making more than twenty steps and her partner, in a leather jacket and jeans, joined her.

She was indelible, like the colour of a dye. Yet it was not she who was that colour, it was her wanting. A question of age? Yes and no. All colours eventually fade, yet mine I hope is still as glaring as hers.

You know the stool on which I sit in front of the mirror to do my hair. It must be at least fifty years old, and the embroidered fabric which covered the seat was worn and faded. On the canvas there were traces, like stains, of the garlands and fruit which once decorated it, but all the coloured silks were worn away. So I decided to have it reupholstered, and carried it to Prem in his little workshop behind the flea market.

Can you upholster a stool for me?

I only do armchairs and sofas.

It's a little stool and I've brought it.

For a stool you have to go to a saddle-maker!

Then he laughed. For you I'd upholster an upright piano! Behind his tinted glasses – he suffers from trachoma – his young eyes were smiling. Upholsterers work a lot by touch.

When I go to fetch the finished stool, he is still smiling. I have a surprise for you, he says. He holds up the old faded fabric of the seat for me to see. Then, in a flash, he turns it round, and there on the back is a tousled mass of silk threads in all their splendour. As though they had been dyed yesterday. Dyed magenta, orange, pomegranate red, scarlet, lemon, pistachio green, kohl black, ivory.

The colours have been preserved, he explains, because they were out of the light – between your arses and the stuffing. I thought you'd like to keep it.

The knots of the threads are like tiny corpuscles. Red, white, copper, topaz. And on many the embroideress left little tails of thread, like hairs, and when I smooth the cloth with the back of my hand, these hairs stand up.

The intensity of such colours contain the secret of procreation. Colours exist to provoke desire. And isn't that why we women embroider? We did embroider before we arranged explosives. Both require enormous patience.

Perhaps this is why the girl dancing to the accordion in the cellar made me think of dyes.

What the young know today they know more vividly and intensely and accurately than anyone else. They are experts of the parts they know. The other part we can show them. Maybe it has always been like this. And what we today can show them is that victory is an illusion, that the struggle will be endless, and that to continue it, aware of this, is the only way to acknowledge the immense gift of life!

Before they took you, I thought little about the future. Our parents might have said the future was what we were struggling for. Not us. We were fighting to remain ourselves.

Since they took you, the future is continually with me, because I'm waiting for you. I imagine the lives of children not yet born. I don't know whether it's my head or my womb which imagines them. Perhaps my breasts.

They are not necessarily our children. Who knows whether I'll have the chance to bear your children? Who knows whether I'll make it through the crack between the concrete floor and the battered metal door of your cell, having first arranged, in my girdle what will explode time.

At the instant before we die, perhaps time makes an about-turn, mi Guapo. Perhaps at that instant looking backwards offers all the promises of the future. Perhaps the past becomes pregnant if the future is barren! Perhaps the worn embroidery is turned over, and we see the silk threads as they are when they first come out of their dye.

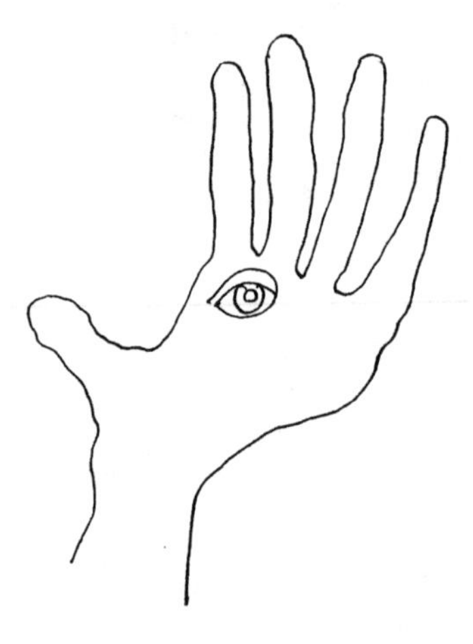

I have sent four packets of Jamaican coffee. Three for them, one for you.

A

The Second Packet of Letters

On the strip of cotton fabric that ties together the packet are the following words, written in an ink that the cloth has somewhat blotted:

It's not that we have hope – we shelter it.

Mi Guapo,

The last darkness of the night. I haven't yet slept. I was thinking about the future. Not any future anywhere. Not our future together. About the future here they're trying to abort. They won't succeed. The future, that they fear, will come. And in it, what will remain of us, is the confidence we maintained in the dark.

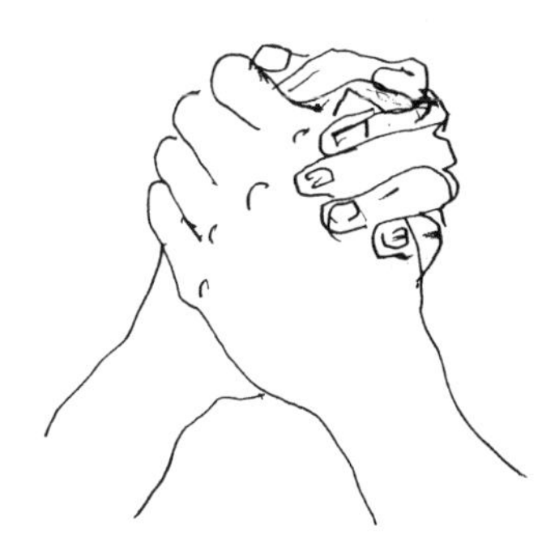

Your A'ida

Ya Nour,

Remember Nininha whom you called Dearest Diplomat? She turned up a week ago with her round face, in her tiny shoes, and with her air, whether sitting or standing, of looking down at the world from a balcony. She brought me some maple syrup, for she'd been in Canada. It's a long while since I saw her, and she's still the same impossible storyteller. She was telling me about an arms-dealer she met in Moscow.

What sort of arms?

She shrugged her shoulders and added that he invited her to Latvia.

Why Latvia, he had business there?

To see the Baltic.

And what did he want from you?

He liked my impersonations.

So you made him laugh?

Not really, he was too nervous and, apart from Russian, he only spoke English.

You speak English well.

No, A'ida, I've forgotten. I spoke English well when I was in Buenos Aires long ago. Nevertheless I made his friends in Riga laugh and he begged me to perform for them time and again.

You stayed long there?

Until he was assassinated.

Assassinated!

I was waiting for him in the swimming pool, Nininha said, and I heard a shot. I waited and waited and he didn't turn up.

So?

I left. I was there only five days.

You know who killed him?

I've no idea.

Immediately I was furious with her. Beside myself. I shouted at her, I think I called her a tart. She was visibly at a loss. I knew I was being unjust yet I couldn't control my anger. I started shaking her, physically with my two hands. My fury wasn't about what she had or had not done, or how she behaved with the Russian in the Riga hotel – that was her affair. It was about what she wouldn't say, about her silences. They enraged me. Secretiveness is a virtue, no question, often indispensable. But Nininha's silences come from despair.

She has come to believe that life is an accident, something that wasn't meant to happen. And so it's better to keep quiet, better to pick up the pieces that remain, stick them together somehow, and say nothing about the rest. Nothing. Nothing! Nothing!

She broke away from me and left without saying another word, leaving the door open behind her. I went and sat on the top of the outside staircase. She had already disappeared. I could hear the eucalyptus tree rustling in the wind, and I asked myself whether I had become so madly angry because I suspected I too could come to believe that life was an accident that wasn't meant to happen. I sat and sobbed; ashamed and sorry for myself.

Two evenings later Nininha knocked on the door. She was smiling and held a finger to her lips to indicate I shouldn't talk. She walked across to the cassette player – it's still in the corner where the photo of the mountain is – and put in a CD. Then she stood there, hands on hips, waiting. A tango, with its blood-beat fatality. She began to dance. She didn't look at me, but her choices of where to advance and step, acknowledged my presence.

Tangos are made up of scraps of life, which have happened to survive. Scraps, rags, gathered together into the zigzag of the legs, continually obedient to flowing blood, spilt or unspilt.

I waited for her to turn and pause, and then I joined her. She flashed me a smile and took hold of me, milonguero style, very close, with our legs free, and she led and I followed. She waited for me and I waited for her. Our bodies were listening to one another. She held nothing back, no silences. Nininha gave of herself totally which meant I did the same, and together, like the two pieces which make a pair of scissors, we cut. Cut making a seamless garment which was meant to happen.

You know what I'm going to cut for you?

I love you. A.

"No history is mute. No matter how much they own it, break it, and lie about it, human history refuses to shut its mouth. Despite deafness and ignorance, the time that was continues to tick inside the time that is."

Galeano told us. Eduardo, thank you.

Mi Guapo,

He was thirteen, perhaps fourteen. He already had a man's voice but not the pace of a man's voice. Raf was in pain and determined not to show it. K. and two other kids had knocked on my front door and woken me up. Raf was wounded in the leg and couldn't put his right foot on the ground. They had carried him hobbling, his two arms round their shoulders. His name's Raf, they told me.

Spontaneous courage begins young. What comes with age is endurance – the cruel gift of years.

They shot at him from one of their jeeps; he was out after curfew. He managed to crawl under an abandoned truck and then hide in a ruin. I told the kids I would examine him alone in the pharmacy. That way if the lights there attracted attention – it was past midnight – they wouldn't be implicated.

We fetched a stretcher from the shop, laid Raf on it, carried him back along the broken road and then shifted the stretcher on to the sickbed that's permanently in the pharmacy's back room. He'd apparently lost a fair amount of blood.

I told K. he could come back in an hour or so if he wanted, and if, by any chance, he found the pharmacy without lights and bolted, it would mean I had taken Raf urgently to the hospital.

The three of them stared at me as if I'd become

immensely large. Probably won't be necessary, I said reassuringly, I'll do our best to avoid it, but we have to imagine everything, don't we? If we're here, you knock three times on the door.

When we were alone, Raf smiled at me. Strange smile for someone so young – as if we had both, the two of us, qualified for something, and the smile was its proud acknowledgement.

They shot five rounds and I think three missed, he said.

Where's your mother?

In the village.

What are you doing here?

Working.

You work late!

You're working late too, he replied, and he screwed up his eyes. I wasn't sure whether in pain or as a sign of conspiracy. Perhaps both.

I eased off his jeans, swabbed his leg and cut with scissors the tourniquet at the top of his thigh. There was no sudden surge of blood so the artery, thank God, was untouched. He was watching me, curious, but not about his immediate condition: You know what I'm dreaming about? he asked.

I tested his reactions by scratching the sole of his dusty bloodstained foot and his leg twitched as it should. Its nerves were functioning. I washed his feet.

You know what I'm dreaming about? he repeated.

No, tell me. I'm going to examine your wound now, if it hurts too much you whisper to me.

I'm dreaming, he said, of lying on the deck of a

motor-launch and you're driving it, and we are far from the coast and the boat's thumping the waves. Thump. Thump.

There were two wounds which were adjacent. One was long and not very deep and the other was ugly and small and profound. My guess was that the bullet, which caused the first, had entered at a tangent, because shot from above, and had re-emerged where the wound ended above the knee.

In the ugly wound there was probably a bullet. I stepped across to the analgesics to find the diamorphine I was looking for.

Don't go, he whispered.

You think I'd leave you on the deck? I'm going to give an injection into the top of your arm.

I did so, (5 mg.) and we both waited.

Where's our boat going? I ask him as I pick up with my left hand the little clip instrument for holding open the lip of a wound. The *bank* of a wound as the French say, like a river bank.

In my right hand I have a canulla and with its tip I tap very gently along the length of the shallow gash, waiting to hear a metallic click, or to touch suddenly the hardness of metal. You're more likely to register an embedded bullet like this than to see it with your eye.

You tell me where we are going, he says, I'm on my back on the deck and you're steering. Where are we heading?

There is no bullet. I let the lip fall back. Now for the ugly one.

You know something about the dreams of men, all of you men? I ask him.

Tell me, he says gruffly.

You love dreaming of comfort . . .

I'm probing and I think I hear the click of metal. I tap twice more. A bullet.

And women what do they—? Abruptly he clenches his teeth.

We'll wait a moment.

So what do women dream of? he eventually asks.

Of places no longer being separated, I tell him.

Places have to be separated, it's what kilometres are for!

The quiet logic of his reply reminded me so much of you that I had to bite my lip.

Don't look now, I whispered, shut your eyes.

With my eyes shut I get scared, I see their Uzis pointing straight at me.

Then look at my face not my hands.

So you have dimples! he said, you still have dimples.

From the bottom of the wound I extracted with the forceps a greenish bullet like a rotten tooth. He didn't so much as flinch. Next I dripped betadine into the wound until it overflowed like a volcano does. He clenched his right fist, nothing more.

Picking up, with a pair of tweezers, the 30 mm Uzi bullet, I showed it to him.

And he began to sob. I put my head beside his, and after a few minutes he fell asleep.

I close his wounds with thread and a tiny crescent needle. After each stitch has brought the two banks of the river together, I circle with the thread around the tweezers that are holding the needle, to make a knot. And knot by knot

I proceed. The flesh wants to be joined. I fix two dressings, I place a pillow under his head. And I rock the stretcher in imitation of a boat riding the swell of the waves.

It was 2.30 am. We were alone, we were waiting. It was quiet. I hoped you were asleep.

[Letter unsent]

Mi Soplete,

I'm arranging things in boxes: bowls, cups, scales, splints, syringes, scissors, packets, packets, packing up. How many times have I had to move out in my life? It began in childhood when I thought it was a game, until I saw my mother's tears.

There's a line, if I can remember it. The neighing horses . . . "No widow wants to return to us, there where we have to go, north of the neighing horses . . ."

You are with me wherever I go.

In this shop which we have to leave, Idelmis was dispensing medicines and offering tips to those in pain and praying, with her forehead clenched, before I was born. She wore long dresses which came down to her ankles and they had floral patterns as if they too were some kind of herbal recipe. It was I who introduced the white overall.

And now by the end of this month we have to shut up shop and move out. For her it's hard. No point in taking them, she said about the snakes last week. I know what it's like to lose your mind, she complained this morning, leaving here I'm losing my mind.

I know I'm life for you, and the pain of it, and its joy.

Idelmis could retire and sell the business, and she doesn't want to. The scientist in her knows it would be reasonable and seeks my support. You could manage better without me. And the sorceress in her refuses and turns her back. We'll know when the time comes, she says.

If she didn't hand over cures and palliatives and prescriptions of hope and warnings, what would happen to her? She'd go lame, she'd sit in her room counting, she'd become a widow for a second time, and disappear behind the neighing horses.

It's not myself I hand over to you in your cell tonight – that would be too simple – what I hand over to you is yourself, yourself loved in every part.

The shop we're moving to is five minutes away, near the ice-cream factory. It was once a grain merchants. Then a draper's. I will die in you and if you die before me, you will call me. We have to empty the pull-out drawer cabinets with all the medicines in alphabetical order in them, so they can be taken apart and reinstalled in Sucrat.

Here they're going to build a tower of corporate offices and the passageways and lean-to dwellings and cared-for corners will all be bulldozed out of existence.

Belladonna, hawthorn, ibuprofen, lysine, paracetamol, theophylline, valerian . . .

This afternoon I said something without thinking, and it changed Idelmis' mood in a flash. For the first time for a month her eyes sparkled, and she lifted up a hand, its fingers playing an invisible flute in the air . . .

Let's arrange this shit differently in Sucrat, I said. What are you saying? she grumbled. Simple, I said, we arrange the medicines, in alphabetical order of course, but not according to their form, according to their capacities.

She understood immediately. We wouldn't arrange them according to whether they were pills, powders, capsules, solutions, pomades, creams, etc., but according to their therapeutic categories: cardiology, stomatology, haematology, endocrinology, urology, etc.

I've never seen it done, she said, and why not? Let's do it, it'll work.

What's the difference? you'll ask, and I don't know. All I know is that my whole life has led me to you and that Idelmis before she left this evening was happy.

Is it something to do with how we are made?

Your
A'ida

Sometimes it's hard to find the time between
to tell you what you mean to me
You are the rose of my heart—

Johnny Cash, last night . . .

If you're tired rest your head on my arm
Rose of my heart.

Ya Nour,

You asked me to send some soap – the nearest we can get to swimming, you say. It came this morning, your letter. So I'm sending twelve soaps in the hope you'll get four.

There's the widow called Tamara who comes to the pharmacy from time to time. In her seventies. She came in with a cut on the forefinger of her right hand this morning. Very slight but somewhat infected – it had happened two or three days before, with a knife when she was slicing potatoes.

She shows it to me. She has shown it to nobody else, and by now the two of them – she and the cut – are getting on each other's nerves. I go and fetch some ointment and a little packet of adhesive dressings.

I explain to Tamara how to put one of the dressings on. She imitates my gestures with her left hand and laughs.

Once more, she pleads.

So I show her again, and she imitates me with the concentration of a little girl learning to dress a doll. Her right hand has become her doll, and now she can return alone to her tiny room, with a doll and not a cut.

Thank you, she says after paying, you're an angel.

I shake my head. The angels have gone, I tell her.

Today there's confirmation that our application for a marriage has been turned down. Statute IBEC-27 Clause: F.

There's no larger mistake possible than to believe that

an absence is a nothingness. The difference between the two is a question of timing. (About which they can do nothing.) Nothingness is before and absence afterwards. At times it's easy to confuse the two: hence some of our griefs.

Your
A'ida

Almost all promises are broken. The poor's acceptance of adversity is neither passive nor resigned. It's an acceptance which peers behind the adversity, and discovers there something nameless. Not a promise, for (almost) all promises are broken; something like a bracket, a parenthesis in the otherwise remorseless flow of time. And the sum total of these parentheses is perhaps eternity.

After work this evening I went to see Ariadne in Sayomal, and I picked blackcurrants in her small garden whilst she was washing her hair in a zinc bath. She has much thicker hair than mine – you could hide an army behind it!

They stain your fingers red, the blackcurrents, and their taste, not their colour, is black, black and marine, like the taste of something living on the seabed. A sea urchin or some other echinoderms might have the same taste, though it would be less strong, less pungent. How do I know this? I don't know, mi Guapo, yet I know it.

Remember their smell? The smell of blackcurrants? Particularly the smell of their leaves when the fruit begin to ripen. I adore their smell. I want to bring it into your cell.

There's a variety of white snail who adore it too. You know how many varieties of snail there are? Guess. Thirty-five thousand! I want to bring the smell of blackcurrants into your cell tonight.

These snails are small, the size of my little finger nail. Dozens of them asleep on the leaves, using the leaves as hammocks. Whatever it is they eat there, they've done no apparent damage. Many snails, I remember learning – ah, the things we learn! – many snails eat by scraping with their rough tongues their food off stones and barks. They eat, as it were, off the sidewalks they walk on.

In Ariadne's blackcurrant bush, if each snail ate ten

currants per hour you wouldn't notice it – there are so many!

And this reminds me of a proverb which Dimitri – who has had to stop work on his house through lack of funds – told me yesterday: To take a little from where there's plenty, is not theft, but sharing!

The snails go with what I was telling you about the sea-urchins. Any lifetime is absurdly short compared to the longevity of memory. The echinoderms and gastropods evolved at more or less the same period, long before the mammals. And to you they gave two life sentences!

All day it was hot and oppressive – the kind of weather when I want to send you bottle after bottle of cold water. Later, when I sat on a stool to pick the currants, there was an evening breeze, and the last rays of the sun shone agreeably on my back, and I could feel warm silk across my shoulder blades, and Ariadne was splashing in her tub. We have only one life to live, you and I.

I lift up a branch so I can see all the clusters of berries and I start picking.

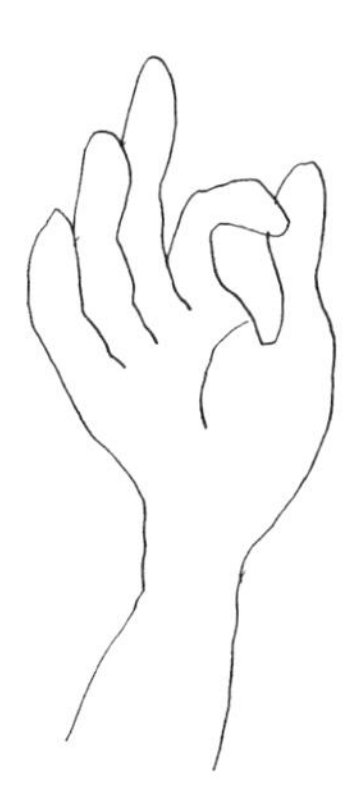

I start milking the bush as if it were a goat.

Berries flow, one by one, from my fingertips down my fingers into the palm of my hand. When I can hold no more, I empty them into a basin and begin again with cluster after cluster, lifting one branch after another.

And the berries dislodge themselves and roll down my fingers into the cup of my hand, as if they were preordained to do just this. A strange sensation. As if, at the touch of my fingertips, their time had come. They made me think of how, at a given moment of the month, an ovum of mine leaves its follicle and falls into the fringe of my tube, whose lashes, like eye lashes, propel it forwards, until it eventually lands in what is called the pavilion at the top of my uterus. Mi Guapo, to you in your cell, I say: this pavilion is your pavilion!

I picked 3 kilos. Enough to make a dozen pots of black currant jelly. Never put too much sugar. Shouldn't crowd out the sea urchins. Heat to 200C.

In each of my ovaries there are two hundred thousand potential ova. And during my lifetime only four hundred will mature. Such is nature's abundance.

I'll make the jelly tomorrow and I'll send you four pots. Three for them and one for you. Her abundance? Better, her determination!

Now you smell my blackcurrants?

Your
A'ida

Poultices of blackcurrant take away the pain of burns.

Palindrome. Writing, offering the same sense whether read from beginning to end, or from end to beginning. According to Yannis, the Greek literally means Return Road.

Palindrome of a day. I am asleep, not the deepest phase yet, for I can still feel the pleasure of welcoming sleep. On the bunk of cell 73, feet pointing SE, I'm waiting for sleep and reviewing the day. Placing a pile of books on the bunk and stepping up on to it with my left foot, my left shoulder leans against the wall – there's a polished spot on the wall where my sleeping shirt touches and rubs against it every night – for like this I can see the sky, otherwise I can't. Clear stars waiting tonight. Orion's Belt. NNE.

Take off trousers. Take off boots. Untie them. Sit on bunk. Brush teeth whilst avoiding looking into mirror. For some reason they tolerate a mirror and not bottles. When I wake and get up I look into the mirror and say Good Morning. I never say Good Night. A superstitious habit ever since I was in cell 73. When I'm transferred, it will change.

Listen to music on my radio. A few times Mozart composed in palindromes. Being escorted along corridor from Common Room, a deserted abattoir corridor. Specialised prison architects were commissioned to design abattoirs. At one point the herder stops and tells me about his son who is 18 and hopes to be a swimming champion. I repeat the word Swimming, for when I say it, I think of you. Listening also to something else from cell 69: an old song with changed words that I reckon is a message.

In Common Room TV on. Following supper, an animated discussion with Murat, Ali, Jaimes, Kadem about EROEI. Energy Return on Energy Input. Today's capitalism would be impossible without the very high return of the thick energy of fossil fuels, hence the question of what may happen in four decades when oil supplies are exhausted. Will there be only the thin solar energy? Nearest herder on rostrum sits listening, gun across his knees.

What's hallucinating about any TV programme is the extent of the walking space available to the participants. US troops in Iraq apparently using DIME weapons, which inflict internal burns without penetrating flesh. The soup tonight is thin.

Pour from your bottle of olive oil into all the eating bowls I can reach. We have negotiated the right to keep bottles in the Common Room. Their guns are quicker than anything we could cut with broken glass. Consultation with Jaimes about Kadem not eating. It's his third month. It gets easier – slowly each of us learns, in his own way, to move about in time.

Searched when leaving afternoon workshop. Nothing found. Silvio, Samir, Durito and I mending phones, TVs and other hardware. Workshop hours are the ones which happily pass slowest, for we alter the pace as we please and in a strange way the prison authority depends on our cunning as menders.

There are days when we talk little at lunch. Like today.

One hour exercise in yard to get up appetite, 8 new prisoners. Two of us walk behind them for news, warnings and to slip them cash; every bank note is taken away on admission. I receive news about you.

When I enter the yard, I look up at the sky to see what

your weather is like. Nose the sky like it was your armpit. Cruising white clouds moving fast. They disappear before they appear. The more you can't visit, the more I picture you. Around you the non-stop blue. The blue sky above the yard is not indifferent, far from it. It never collaborates with victors, only with the pursued. Recurring thought on first stepping into the yard.

In cell, reading and note-taking. Where there's little else, words count. For the first time the nature of the planet, risks to be treated in its entirety as no more than the simple profit-yielding difference between use value and exchange value. Return escorted to cell from ablutions with mug of coffee and bread. Hold out empty mug for coffee.

Dry my own body slowly. Wash my body. Waiting outside cell door, clothes over my arm until ablutions contingent with herder arrive.

Am awake.

Hellish racket of the Banging-up. For an infinitesimal moment I don't know where I am. I'm asleep.

Hayati,

A red washing-up bowl between my feet and I'm sitting on the roof in what you call the fourth room. From the corner sweetmeats shop in the street below, wafts the smell of burnt vanilla. An evening smell. One never comes across it in the morning. It's already 8.30 pm, and people are still choosing to walk on what was the shady side of the street. Two martins fly between the roofs. Of all I can see at this moment I know it's they who would give you the most pleasure. The sight of them.

With the red plastic bowl I climb across two roofs to Ramon's where there's a tap, and there I fill the bowl up with stolen water. I come back, take off my sandals and put my left foot into the cool water.

Maybe my foot in the water gives you as much pleasure as the martins? I'm teasing you! No better way of passing the time when waiting, Manda says. Teasing makes time trip up, she says.

With both feet in the bowl I feel hobbled. So I take out my left, which is cool now, and put in my right. It's from their feet you can best guess somebody's age. Mine included.

Earlier this evening Ama was up here. As thin as a reed. She was watching me from her window and then she stepped out, sat down beside me and whispered: I want to tell you something odd!

Funny or sinister?

Upsetting, she says. Then waits.

Go on.

Last night I saw a film on TV at a friend's place, she went on. Nothing special, an Argentinian film I guess, but the actor who played the main male role, was Rami's double. I'm telling you. Everything about him was Rami! I said to myself it's him! He twists his neck in the same way. He walks and coughs in the same way. He takes off his shoes in the same way. He's going bald in the same way. I went crazy watching the film because it couldn't have been Rami. He's dead and he never played in any film.

Ama begins to catch her breath. What I couldn't take – she spits the words out – I couldn't take it that there were two Ramis. If he isn't unique, he isn't dead!

There's sweat on her lip and chin. This means, she says, don't you see? This means Rami died for nothing! She leans her head against mine.

Now, I have to explain. Ama met Rami last winter. A man about ten years older than her. He was an electrician and an ace with computers. I only saw him once. Very proud moustache and laughing eyes. Ama was a little in love with him. If there's such a thing as being a little in love? Perhaps its a question of volume, she could have turned the volume up higher! She didn't.

Four months ago, Rami was killed, hauled out of bed by a patrol, taken to the River Zab and shot. Ama was only informed three days later when his body was found.

I knew it before they told me, she explained to me after

she'd heard the news of his death. I knew it the night they shot him. I suddenly woke up and there was this bottomless well inside my ribs. I felt it. I couldn't throw myself into it, because I was it! The blessing, she went on after a very long pause, is that I hadn't yet got used to him. He was new. I wailed out of pity for him, out of pity and fury and I prayed for him, but not for myself. I knew I still had a sack full of other things to pick up in life, to take, to love and to lose, one by one.

She was far calmer that evening when she heard the disastrous news than she was tonight. Tonight she screamed across the rooftops. How's it possible, she screamed at the sky, how's it possible that there are two Ramis?

Come and sit, I told her.

She looked at me hard with her semi-permanent smile. OK, she said, if he'd been a twin born of the same mother, but he wasn't!

She walked to the edge of our roof, muttering to herself: If there wasn't only one Rami, if Rami wasn't unique, then he isn't dead! How can I mourn him if he isn't, isn't unique? And I need to mourn him!

She sat down and howled with grief, deep grief. Tears and sweat shiny on her thin face. She's twenty years old. We waited together. Then I threw out the water from the red washing-up bowl and went to refill it from Ramon's tap, and brought it back and placed it by our feet.

Take off your sandals, I told her.

If you do, she said.

It's too small for both our feet.

My right foot and your left foot, she said, and then she

stopped smiling and sprinkled water on her face from her hand.

This is what I had to tell you tonight.

Your A.

The day that hunger disappears the world will see a spiritual explosion such as humanity has never known, Lorca said to Jaimes a while ago.

Ya Nour,

Last week I saw Alexis. We played several hands. He was my partner and straightaway we merged three melds because we had only two wild cards. He brought me almonds that I can't stop eating. We've been cut off from supplies. Listen, I'll bite one, hear my tooth crack it?

As a child I thought almonds were like no other nut or fruit because I was convinced they were handmade. Today I know they contain soluble protein and that the bitter, as distinct from the sweet variety contains hydro-cyanic acid, the catalyst used for extracting gold and other pure metals from their ores, and, sometimes, for filling the little phial which can save us, when captured, from fates worse than death.

I knew, of course, about almond trees with their white blossoms. Bridal white, and I dreamt of being married with those flowers in my hair. Today I dream of being married (they have knocked back our third application) in the parlour of Suse prison!

I knew about the trees, yet when I arranged the nuts in circles on the tabletop, I told myself that, long ago, it was a woman who had thought them up as a sweetmeat. Very long ago. She was a goddess, not a woman. A sweetmeat for her sweetheart. She concocted the first almond, tasted it, reduced the sugar, added oil, tasted it again, nodded, added a touch of cumin, and decided almonds were what she would make for her lover's return.

So, she gave instructions to a tree. It was the first graft, made with words, not with a cutting and rags. The next Spring the tree flowered and produced in June abundant almonds with the same taste as the one I'm biting now. Later the goddess's lover sailed away, never to return, and she grafted on to a second tree instructions for the bitter almond whose blossom is pinker, for it is mixed with drops of blood from a broken heart.

Hydro-cyanic acid is also an antispasmodic. Used for injections to lower high blood pressure in extremis.

And Alexis told me a story. Now I've heard the story from four men all of whom were there in the brig. When the other three tell it, they say it was you who started to bark, as a protest against insults being hurled at a new arrival, an old man, by a herder who was banging him up in the slot next to yours. When you told it, I remember well, you said it was the old man who started to bark.

Knowing what it's like being transferred to an unfamiliar prison, I think you invented the barking for him! I'm almost sure you did. It takes an hour or two to get your breath, after the unfamiliar door is dubbed up in the familiar way, whilst you stand there facing it! Facing it! Tongue behind the teeth.

In any case, the companeros on the other side of the old man's slot picked it up and barked and the bark went to the next slot and the next and the next, one after another, not hurrying, until the whole tier was barking.

And it wasn't any bark, Alexis insists. It was the bark of

a hunting dog. Hunting dogs bark as they run, they bark to give news to the rest of the pack. They don't just announce their presence and yap like terriers. They listen to one another, they respond, they imitate, they close in.

The herders started to shout, to threaten, to bang on the doors. They took out their shit-sticks. They set off alarms. To no effect. The barking continued and unlike the racket the herders were making, the barking was sure of itself and calm. It passed from tier to tier until the whole brig was barking.

Then, at a certain moment the barking changed and became deeper and more intimate, it became a chuckling bark because everybody recognised the herders were scared.

They had all the usual controls at their fingertips, and yet fear was touching them, along their backs, down their spines. They were being brought up short by the extent of what they could not control. And as soon as this was evident, they saw the unchanging fact of being outnumbered as a threat. They began to count and recount the bodies. They glanced swiftly at one another for reassurance.

And how long did it go on? I asked you. You shrugged your shoulders. And I knew why you did so. You did so because you wanted to say: All night! And to say so would have been a gross exaggeration and, at the same time, God's truth. He often exaggerates!

Eventually you all decided – at the same moment – to stop barking, not one of you, not even the most inveterate loner was tempted to break the ensuing silence. You all knew that for once the silence belonged, not to them, the herders, but to you, the barkers. And this is why the barking lasted all night!

Telling it again, I love you all, and I send you what I send you.

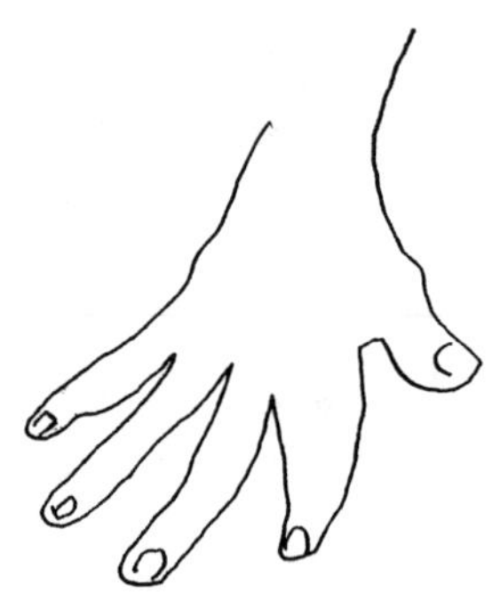

You can put it wherever you like.

Your

A'ida

On the radio a recording of Mussorgsky's Tableaux d'une Exposition. *Quite long. Over half an hour. A good number of silences, I didn't count them. Never heard it before. Anyway, never listened to it before. This time, yes. Next morning Murat told me he listened too. We both had the same reaction which made us laugh when we exchanged it. Precisely the same.*

M.'s composition is meant to have been inspired by the composer's walk through an exhibition of paintings. Doubtless some of the tunes were already in his head. (I looked him up in the prison library encyclopaedia and he was thirty-five when he wrote it, seven years before he died of alcohol and epilepsy.) The walk through the exhibition, though, gave him the rhythm he needed.

Yet for Murat and me, for us two, what the piano was playing was a prisoner's walk from the prison after his release. The small door in the large prison door had shut behind him and he was striding along the street towards town.

He's taking in scenes of daily life such as he hasn't witnessed since he was hooked and sentenced, and the music is following the rhythm of his walking. Or, to be more exact, the rhythm and melodies of the piano which change according to what he's passing in the street yet continually return to the rhythm of release, is exactly how we, still inside, picture stepping out and going to town, when, and if, our break should come. Pass the word to other brigs.

My welder.

I found a book about turbojet engines. It was in the pocket of a jacket you used to wear. And the jacket was above the rafters in the compañero's bedroom as you call it. You stuffed it there to keep the north wind out.

I pulled it down because I remembered it, and I needed a large button for a coat I'm making for Sahar. You got the book when you were in Carthage. It's in French and belongs to the collection: *Que Sais-Je.*

The name of the collection made me smile then, and it still does years later. We know everything we need to know but it doesn't fit into words! What we don't know and will never know is what is going to happen next.

I take up the book and it falls open at a diagram drawn on a blank page by you. Under the drawing you wrote the name of the parts in your own handwriting. And it suddenly strikes me I'm looking at a love poem! "Moteur de lancement et excitatrice > génératrice > chambre de combustion > turbine" !

A love poem! This is what prolonged chastity does to the imagination!

I cut off the buttons.

Your

Acetylene

Mi Guapo,

When I was a small girl I had a collection of feathers. Nearly 200. From 27 species. Each bird had its own envelope. We haven't talked much about our childhoods, have we? It's something I look forward to us doing, inshallah. People talk about their childhoods when they fall in love and we didn't talk Why do you think that was? I think I know but I can't find the words. I'll find them when you come out. It was this collection of feathers, bird's feathers, that first got me interested in angels. I learnt about cherubim, seraphim, the fallen ones and the special messengers. Each category of angel had different wings, a different way of folding them when not flying and, naturally, different feathers.

Whenever I ran a fingertip along the length of one of my bird feathers, I made a wish. By the time I was studying pharmaceutics at the Institute in Tarsa the angels and I had parted company. But these days I've been thinking something else and I want to tell you what I've been thinking in a letter one day.

Long ago I used to think the nearest to the eternal is the sense of blessedness which arrives after making love. I'd say now it's the hearing of a certain sort of rumour, a street rumour, which starts in the future when the streets will be paved, the guns will be kept at home, and fathers will teach arithmetic to their sons.

Your A'ida

Hell was the invention of money-makers; its purpose was to divert the attention of the poor from their present afflictions. Firstly with the repeated threat that they might be very much worse off. And secondly with the promise, for the obedient and loyal that, in another life, in the Kingdom of God, they would all enjoy what wealth can buy in this world and more.

Without the evocation of Hell, the Church's demonstrative wealth and ruthless power would have been far more openly questioned because they were in evident contrast to the teaching of the Gospels.

Hell bestowed a kind of sanctity on amassed wealth.

The inflictions of today have gone further. No need to evoke a Hell in the afterlife. A hell for the excluded is being constructed in this one, announcing the same thing: that only wealth can make sense of being alive.

Mi Guapo,

One by one small birds appear on the bare branches of the apple tree behind the old draper's shop, which has been transformed and where the medicines have been delivered, unpacked and arranged in drawers and on shelves in their new order. The floor area is a bit larger than in the old pharmacy. I'd say at least half of one tier in the prison of Suse. The problem is that the new shop isn't easy to find, for the road has been destroyed. When clients come through the door, many of them whistle and blow out air from their mouths, saying: Never thought I'd find you! Now I know, thank God! You're on the edge of the world!

To which Idelmis replies: Who'd want to be at the centre of today's world! What are you complaining about? Been to a doctor? Or you need a home cure? Home is the code-word she has taken to using, and it refers to ancient, herbal medicines.

She also tells them, when possible, about a generic medicine with a different name to the one prescribed. She calls them competitive cures. Competitive? Produced by another big firm to undercut another. Just the same and just a little cheaper, take it if it's not too dear.

The pharmaceutical firms produce a certain number of medicines for animals, particularly dogs. And on the boxes of the dog medicines the prescribed dosage is printed in letters and also in braille, so that the blind owner of a guide dog can read it, should his or her dog fall ill. Thoughtful, farseeing ... Yet on a packet of Humira – for polyarthritis (costing over a thousand dollars) the dosage and necessary precautions are meticulously printed, and not a word is said about how to acquire or steal the money to pay for it, or its generic!

Idelmis has survived the upheaval of the move better than I feared. And my idea of arranging the medicines according to their pharmaceutical function challenges and intrigues her. It wouldn't be easy for a beginner, but she's an old hand and she strides around, treating the whole shop as if it were a chart to navigate by – she's become like a ship's captain pacing her bridge. Maybe I should buy her a cap! She sails in five seconds from the continent of rheumatology to the continent of endocrinology with its hormone rivers. She can pilot to any small island – for example the isle of anti-inflammatories non-steroid. Without realising what I was doing, I've presented her with a ship! Her table and chair, where she sits and reads when not serving at the counter, she has placed in the straits of the voice: oto-rhino-laryngology. Meanwhile, in the pharmacy freezer I have a stock of ice-creams (lemon, mango, redcurrant, orange) and every afternoon at six I hand one to her. She licks it standing in the doorway, looking across the waste land towards the ice-cream factory. Routine helps.

Come back to the birds on the bare branches of the apple tree. I was staring at the tree before opening the shop this morning, and I was thinking about the missile that brought such havoc a week ago. Amongst others, Gassan the barber's house was destroyed.

One by one the birds appeared; they didn't fly into the tree, they appeared on its branches like prayers. Gassan's house was destroyed by a missile, aimed, they claim at a hide-out! The birds perched there on the branches of the apple tree like answers, answers to questions which have no words. Watching the birds, I finally cried.

Gassan wasn't there when his house was destroyed. He had gone to the market and was playing cards with some cronies. When he heard the news, he foundered and fell to the floor, making no sound.

The next day I accompanied him to the ruin. There were several epicentres where everything had been reduced to dust, surrounded by tiny fragments. Except for pipes and wires no recognisable objects remained. Everything which had been assembled during a lifetime had gone without trace, had lost its name. An amnesia not of the mind but of the tangible.

He walked several hundred metres down the road to one of the ancient ruins, where a window-frame was still a window-frame, even if there was no glass, and a chair was still a chair with two legs missing. There he found in an outhouse what he was looking for – a broom.

Then we returned to what a few days before had been his home and he began to sweep, looking not at his feet but into the distance. My instinct was not to interfere, and to treat him as if he were a sleepwalker. I'm not sure how long it went on. It covered a lifetime.

He was sweeping in the same place – without moving his feet. At last he paused and looked at me, and this is what he said: I always swept up the hairs on the floor after every customer. It was one of the first rules of the trade you learnt as a barber.

I took his arm, he still held the broom. Perhaps give him valerian officinalis I was saying to myself. This was my trade response to his destitution. How tiny our trades are!

In the dark folds of time maybe there's nothing except the dumb touch of our fingers.

And our deeds.

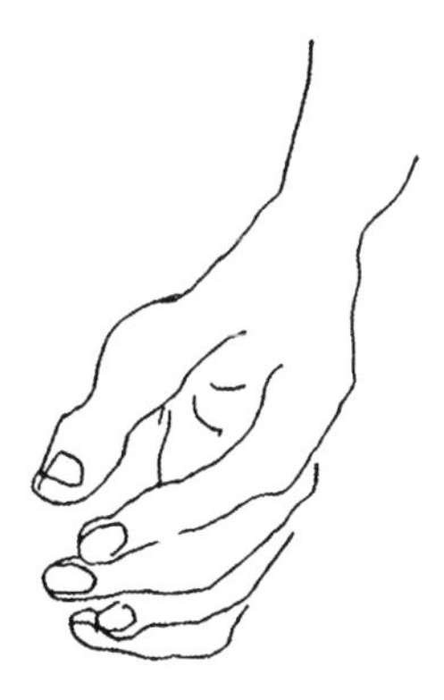

Your A'ida

Dream: The universe was open like a book. Me looking at it. The top right-hand corner of the right-hand page was folded inwards to mark the place. And on that small triangle of folded paper was written the secret of materiality – which was as elegant and faultless as a fractal.

In the dream I was so reassured by this, so happy, that I didn't think of writing it down.

Hayati,

It's happened twice. Yesterday was the second time. I take the Tora Pass to go to Quart. When I get to the top I stop, because I love that view – the hills are like the sheets of a bed somebody's just jumped out of – and because we often stopped there. On the left stands a stone building with a door that doesn't shut and, further on, there's a small farm with goats and washing on the line. Several children, I guess from the washing, but none visible. I stand by the empty stone building looking across the hills to the distant river and a dog approaches me. Size of a terrier, friendly. Noses my hand, tail revolving like an egg whisk. Suddenly he hears something I don't hear and he runs round the building. Several times. Then he vanishes. Returning to the car, I pass the doorway and glimpse inside. There he is, furiously copulating with a bitch, whitish in colour and larger than him. I watch. Nothing will stop him, I think he's like water until it finds sea level. And I drive off, in a better humour than I was before.

Yesterday – and fourteen months have gone by – I take the same road and stop in the same place. And believe it or not, the same dog is there! I have the sense that he almost recognises me. I sit down on a low boulder. He settles on the ground by my feet, tail thumping on the grass. After a while he gets up and leaves. I look across the hills to the river. I watch the clouds. And then abruptly a premonition interrupts me. I know what is going to happen. I know it with such a certainty. I know it as if it were the direct consequence of a deliberate choice on my part.

I get to my feet. I walk towards the farmhouse where the washing was. I walk down a slope where there are many rocks, and there on the wild grass between two boulders the dog is copulating. Not with the same bitch – this one is darker and smaller. In her throat yelps of delight.

I hurry back to the car, trembling. When I'm in the driver's seat, I put my forehead against the steering wheel and I weep. I weep. I fell asleep weeping. I don't know for how long. A passing lorry woke me . . .

[Letter unsent]

I'm sitting at Idelmis' table. The pharmacy is open til midnight for emergency medicines today. It's very quiet. A lorry has just left the ice-cream factory. You've been escorted back to your cell. I get up, walk to the door, open it to watch the night sky, with the idea that I may be doing this at the same moment as you are standing on your pile of books to do the same thing. I ask myself what the night sky offers us? I don't think it's a promise, it's more immediate. Something like a clear conscience? I want you to sleep deeply. It's very cold.

I make coffee and there's a ring at the door. An elderly man whom I don't know. He told me his wife had burnt herself whilst cooking on an open fire. He was breathing as though he'd been running. How long ago? I asked. About an hour, he replied, a neighbour brought me in a car.

Where is your wife burnt?

On her right hand and on her face.

Her face?

Yes, she lurched forward as she was testing the potatoes with a fork.

Has her skin peeled off?

No, it's red and she has blisters.

When he said this, he screwed up his eyes.

Did you put on cold water immediately?

I put her arm in a bucket of water and I put a soaked towel on her face.

Cold water, cold water, cold water, I repeated, is good.

He'd come by car yet in his mind he was running – hence his heavy breathing – to catch up with the burns which had come so fast and unpredictably to afflict his wife.

Her hand is the worst. What can you give for her now?

I'll give you a spray to ease the pain (silver sulphur dioxide), some gauze dressings for her hand, and a disinfectant (laidocaine). As soon as you return home you have to do something else, I told him, you have to take a needle and you have to prick where she's got burnt. Don't prick the blisters. If it hurts her, and she feels pain, it's a good sign, the best sign, for it means the burn is not deep. If it doesn't hurt her, we have to get her somehow to hospital as soon as possible.

May God not want it.

Probably he doesn't.

When the old man leaves, collar up and wrapped in a scarf, his breathing is more regular, and he walks slowly to the neighbour's car, as if for the moment he is ahead of her burns.

Sitting here writing to you, I'm surrounded by extractions, concoctions, herbs, cures, poisons, each in its packet with precise instructions about its proper use, and all of them intended to reduce suffering. Meanwhile there are pains we don't want to reduce! Maybe this is something else the night sky recalls to us.

There were a hundred of us at Vera's funeral. Vera the martyr. Many words honoured her, her parents were aghast and proud. Her body was already pure and she could be buried in her clothes. Several of us washed our faces with the sand beside the grave into which she was lowered. None of us wept.

Afterwards we sat in Issa's place talking about her. Talking about her even when we were silent. You can talk about the dead silently, and maybe the dead feel more at home in the silent talk. Vera is dead, gone. Nothing prepares us for the gone-ness.

We sat in a tight circle and her gone-ness was its centre. It was as geometric as that. We had walked away from her grave three hours before, and it felt like three months. No detail is blurred; simply, so much happened during those three hours. Every few minutes there was one of us who discovered yet another thing that had gone, gone with her, and for which, henceforth, we would have to depend on ourselves alone. This is why we huddled in a circle.

Very soft tap at the door whilst I was writing. Followed by something like a scratching. Might be a dog. Got up to shout: Is there anyone there? Stupid question; it should have been: Who's there?

I'm sick! came the reply. I opened. An unknown young man, thin, with sand on the shoulders of his coat, and a little on his closely cropped hair – as though he had fallen.

As soon as he saw me he began to shout in anger. Why didn't you open when I knocked? I've been waiting for hours! Hours in the cold I tell you! The more he shouted, the more pointed his anger. You don't have the right to be wearing that white coat! he screamed at me. Then he pitched forward on to the floor.

I knelt down to look closer, imagining perhaps a wound.

Looking me in the eye, he whispered: Diabetic! and passed out. I slapped his face. It made no difference. Was his sugar-count too high or too low? Hyperglycaemia or hypoglycaemia? I had to choose between giving him insulin or sugar. I opted for the second because of his inexplicable anger, and if he was suffering from hypoglycaemia I had to be quick – a minute counted.

I fetched half a tumbler of warm water, threw in five lumps of sugar and quickly stirred until they were dissolved. Then I raised his head and eased his mouth open, whilst praying. I changed position, put the head on my lap and rubbed the Adam's apple. He swallowed. Once, twice, three times.

Looking through the door at the stars, I acknowledge at this moment that life is sugar, nothing but, sugar! He opens his eyes.

In a couple of minutes he was back on his feet. He said he had been thrown off a bus and had lost his luggage. As he was unforthcoming, I didn't question him further.

Let me do a blood test, I suggested. He pulled a wad of bank notes out of his pocket and said he needed to buy insulin and a hyperglycaemia reader.

When I had fetched what he needed, he pricked a fingertip and carefully deposited a drop of his blood on the BM stick. We both waited to see what colour the little circle, the size of a ladybird on the stick, would change to. To our surprise it became almost white; his sugar count was normal.

It would seem, he said, that I owe you a word of thanks. He had a foreign accent but, again, I didn't question him.

Everything about him was reluctant and precise, as

though he had learnt that whatever was openly and boldly said, was bound to be false.

I accompanied him to the door and watched him cross the wasteland. He walked like an habitual survivor without glancing back.

As I was telling you– before he interupted us – at Issa's place we kept on sitting there in a circle, recalling Vera's voice, her earrings, the way she held a gun like it was a bouquet, her laugh, her habit of burying her fist in her thick hair and tugging at it when she was impatient, her migraines, her love of pineapples. Finally we fell silent. We had been sitting there for many hours.

It was Issa who finally broke the silence. Soon, he said, alone or together, we'll be going to many different places, and Vera will already be there at each place! And every time she'll leave before we can see her, even if we arrive early!

When Issa said this, I wept. I wept for hours.

I heard a saying once and it impressed me more than a marriage vow. I don't know where it came from. Perhaps, because of the river in it, it came from [here the ink is smudged, the word illegible]. If you go upriver, it said, pick me a flower, if you die before me, wait just beyond the grave.

That's what I need to tell you tonight, mi Kanadim . . . if you go upriver . . . I stayed here to finish this letter and it'll soon be dawn. Now I'll lock up the pharmacy, and walk home under the icy sky that'll be changing.

Your

A'ida

"Only for the powerful is history an upward line, where their today is always the pinnacle. For those below, history is a question which can only be answered by looking backwards and forwards, thus creating new questions . . ."

Marcos.

My welder,

Once upon a time I thought friends who kept cats were a little lazy and a trifle smug. Rather than have a cat sleeping at my feet, I preferred to have something else, very different, under my pillow – or under ours!

Of course I stroked cats, of course I liked to hear them purring, of course I knew they had nine lives and were waiting to be fed by our great-grandparents. Yet today, I told myself, there's no place for cats. Place not time, for cats slip through time unnoticed. No place.

And now I've had a white cat for ten days – maybe two weeks. It happened like this. Wedad had to cross the ocean (why is a long story that I'll tell you when we are sitting by the sea watching our children build sandcastles) and so she asked me if I would look after Coing.

I'll be back in three days, it's not for long, Wedad said. I said OK and now there seems to be no way she can get back.

As soon as I open the door, Coing is there. She follows me from corner to corner. She sleeps beside me on the divan. When she's relaxed she spends hours attending to her toilette. Dirty cats are like drunkards, my aunt used to mutter. She is learning how to live with me. At night she jumps up on to the divan only after I switch off the light, never before. When I put a plate for her on the floor, she noses it and then demonstrably waits – waits for me to sit down at the table – before she starts eating. She knows before I do, when I'm going to get up and drink from the tap.

She has her own special toilette ritual. She licks persistently one held-up white paw until it's shiny with her spit, then she moves her face away sideways and rubs one side of her neck and later one side of her shoulder against the held-up paw that doesn't budge. It's there like a hitching post for horses. Afterwards she repeats the exercise with her other front paw that doesn't budge. And I watch. Do you know what I watch? I watch your absence washing itself with its rough tongue.

Played yesterday. Eight of us. In last game Red Three turned up first on Discard Pile so pile was frozen and we won.

A'ida

For almost two months they have withheld letters. This afternoon during the workshop Durito offered me a reproduction he has on the wall of his cell. Keep it, he said, till her letters come thru' again, they will. Tonight it's on my wall between the mirror and Australia. A painting by Georges de La Tour of a young woman visiting a prisoner at night. He's seated in his cell. She's standing. In her right hand she's holding a candle by the light of which they can examine one another. They're too interested to smile. With her left hand she's just been frisking his hair.

With what I'm sending you today, I want to take you inside my mouth.

You and I are walking down the hill past the mulberry tree. It's been hot all day, the clouds are low, white, friendly. We've just passed on our left the shop that sells shoes, bags and – we always laughed about this – lampshades! After about fifty metres we come to a newly opened grocer's shop. I've noticed it but I've never had time to stop. It belongs to a man who calls himself Garcia. It's a hut with a corrugated roof; he doesn't live there. We go inside. The shop specialises in foodstuffs imported directly from Spain. White beans for example. A whole bin of them. You bury your fist in them, up to your wrist with its whitish scars – then you lift your hand, let the beans run through your fingers and they're as shiny as porcelain. Dried cod. Salado. Strings of sweet red onions.

The owner watches us. We're testing the goods, he's testing us, and we are doing it with smiles. He's a man in his late 60s, with a round face, wearing thick glasses. I ask him how it is he has a direct Spanish connection. My mother lives in Seville. His reply surprises me for she must be of a considerable age. She buys for me, he explains, and she arranges the transport.

You have already strolled out of the shop and are lighting a cigarette, hoping to see a gazelle on the hills towards the east.

Has she ever been here your mother? I ask. She's too old to travel so far, he says, but she's a wonderful buyer. Behind the thick lenses of his glasses his eyes are strange, because they are both concentrated and distant, as though they were looking at two things at the same time – at whatever is in front of him and, simultaneously, at the word or words representing it. I couldn't manage without her, he continues, as women grow older – have you noticed – they forget far less than they did when they were young, and in this they are the opposite of men, with age men forget more and more. I'm already more forgetful than my mother . . . and it's natural.

I disagree and I tell him I already have a good memory!

He makes a gesture with his palms to suggest politely that I'm perhaps no longer young.

Mi guapo, how old are we? We've aged so many times. And will your memory go before mine? Anyway this is all to take you in a minute inside my mouth.

Now he says something else that surprises me. There's nothing like prison, he murmurs, for developing and maintaining memory. You know by experience? I ask quietly. Instead of replying, he enquires whether the move to the new pharmacy went well? He does this to indicate he knows a thing or two about me. Yet as an evasive action, it's also typical of an ex-prisoner.

I look at him hard and in a flash understand his eyes. He is almost blind. I'm sure of it.

You know these? he asks. La Biblia? They are made in Seville. He is holding up a biscuit, wrapped in blue and red and white tissue paper. La Biblia, he repeats, the Bible, because they are like the manna that fell from heaven on to the desert. A manna made from almonds, the sweetest biscuit on earth.

He weighs out 500 gr. of Biblia, slides them into a paper bag and holds it out to me. He weighed them on a pair of scales held in the hand, and he felt where the pointer was with his finger. He didn't use his eyes. I step back.

You can't refuse a gift, he insists, I'm giving them to you.

Why?

I have forgotten, he says, and you have forgotten, perhaps one day we'll ask my mother.

I accept and pay for a string of onions I have chosen.

You are not outside on the road because you never were. You are in your cell no. 73.

So I walk up the hill alone, wondering what you'll make of the story. I have completely forgotten the biscuits.

When I get home I put on some water to boil to make tea and then I remember them. I unwrap one. Oval and the colour of baked bread . The size of a tongue. Yours or mine. Polvoron Artesano de Almendra. A slight smell of cinnamon. Weight: 32 gr. each. I take a small bite for both of us. The baked wheat flour and almond dust, sweet and a little greasy, lines the top of the palette, it sticks to the curved roof of the mouth, whilst below, on the floor, on our tongue lie tiny fragments of roasted nut to shift between the teeth and bite into.

Munching a Biblia is like pulling an almond blanket over our two heads to keep out sand, rain, the wind or the probing searchlight from the mirador.

He gave us 12. 6 for me, 6 for you if they reach you. If they don't, remember I've taken you inside my mouth.

A.

Last week I was in Suse. And I stood under the same street lamps you'll walk under when you come out. Everything looked broken except the miradors and barbed wire. Everything looked makeshift.

All usurpers do their utmost to make us forget that they have only just arrived.

To glimpse the sky I climb above the bunk. The sky a reminder of what may be temporarily forgotten – e.g. the private equity funds available for financial speculation are today worth 20 times more than the sum total of the world's gross national product!

The wind, rendered gently visible by the clouds, is enough to suggest how the time of such illusions is running out.

The Third Packet of Letters

On the strip of cotton fabric that ties together the packet are two words written in smudged ink:

Home Land

Habibi,

When somebody comes into the pharmacy to buy medicines they've been told to take, they're looking for some kind of order, since every complaint is chaotic. In a pharmacy numbers and arithmetic take on once again the no-nonsense neatness they had on the blackboard in school.

How many capsules each dose? How many doses per day? During a meal? Or how long before a meal, or how long after? During how many days? The answers are renumerated several times and written with a ball-point on the packet containing the medicine. I hear people repeating figures to themselves as they go out: two on waking, three during the midday meal, two before bed, repeating them as if they were a telephone number, for like this, my love, the silence of the unpredictable is kept at bay.

A man I didn't recognise was hanging around the back door of the pharmacy. He was wearing a long knitted scarf around his head. In his sixties. Are you looking for something? I asked. May all be well with you and yours, he answered, cardboard boxes! What size? Any size, all sizes, he replied. You're going to make furniture with them? He shook his head, for the first time smiling. Burn them? I'm a storyteller, he said. I'll see what we've got, I said. I came back with a very large box and a good many smaller ones inside it. I thank you. What do you do with them now?

First I pierce holes for air in each one, and then I put a story inside, you should know that stories left in the open fade away, stories need to live in secret but equally they can't live without air . . . What do you really do? I asked. Breed chicks, he said.

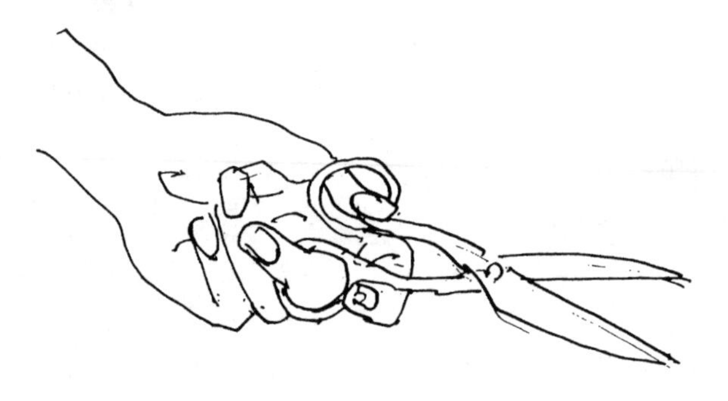

Your pharmacist, whose years are catching up with her, and your

A'ida.

Mi Guapo,

Today I sent you the socks (4 pairs) you asked for. Two pairs with stripes, horizontal, modelling your ankles like the fetlocks of a zebra, and two white pairs without a pattern. I bought them last week and they were in the cupboard with your other clothes. I didn't post them, I sent them with the lawyer, let me know as soon as you get them.

Buttons and beans share something – you know what?

I'll give you a clue. Look at your hands!

You say the drawings of hands I do for you are scotched to the wall directly under the window – like that you say they fly where they want.

They want to touch you, they want to turn your head when you want to look away, they want to make you laugh. What if babies laughed after being delivered instead of crying? Strange question, because we know it wouldn't be life.

In my life though my hands want to make you laugh. Look at your thumbs! They are the connection between the buttons and the beans: whether you're shedding beans from a pod or undoing buttons, your thumbs make almost the same gesture!

This evening I was shedding beans, sitting cross-legged on the roof with Ama. Several kilos. I went up to hang out the washing and there she was with a large basket of beans.

She had begun and hadn't got very far. She looked thinner than ever and her gestures were lackadaisical. I nodded at the beans and remarked like a pharmacist – Rich in proteins and amides! Do them with me, she replied, then we won't starve!

It's not that Ama is idle but maybe with me sitting beside her the coming winter seemed more likely, more probable to her.

I sat down beside her and she began to work quickly. After we'd emptied each pod we threw it into a bucket which is always up there on the roof. Everyone uses it instead of a watering can. She'd fetched it and put it at her feet. The pods of this bean variety are whitish with flecks of brown and grey. Thrown into the bucket they have the colour of old bandages. The swallows are flying low, the air is dusty. Everything waiting for rain. From time to time we looked into one another's eyes and didn't speak. We heard the siren of an armed jeep.

I hope, Ama whispered, I never give birth, to bring another soul down to this earth is a cruelty.

You think you are pregnant?

She shook her head.

There was a white metal washing-basin between us to flick the brown red beans into.

She went on talking: the other day I met Rami's elder brother and he offered me a book he had found when sorting out Rami's few things after his death. I told him I didn't want to know. Ama shook her head.

At first the beans when we unbuttoned them had zinged against the metal of the basin but now they were falling silently into it because it was more than half full. They are of the variety that some people call Cocks' Kidneys.

And so, Ama went on, Rami's brother explained to me that Rami had written my name in the book and must have been thinking of giving it to me as a present. I took it. I have it in my room. It's a book of poems written by a woman called Bejan Matur.)

Ama got to her feet, crossed the roof and came back holding a book. When she was seated again, she opened it and read out loud, quietly and slowly as if she were whispering a prayer.

> The blood that knows how to wait
> also knows how to be a stone

I stopped shedding the beans. Ama looked down into her lap. We waited. Then she read again.

> The blood that knows how to wait
> also knows how to be a stone
> To be in the world is pain
> This I have learned.

She closed the book and placed it next to the bucket.

Why so much pain? she asked me. Everything is pain, why? Men never stop ripping each other to pieces. Tell me. I have to know why. Why are we only born to suffer. This I have learned. I have to know why.

I put my hand into the washing basin of red beans and let them run between my fingers. One evening this autumn,

I told her, we'll let them simmer for seven hours, no salt until they're cooked. We'll have to find some limes – they're better than lemons. And you'll hard boil some eggs – at least six hours in water with onion skins and you won't forget the spoonful of olive oil to stop the water boiling away, will you?

She looked up, leant towards me and kissed me on the mouth. I buried my hand in her thick hair, tugging at it gently. And in doing this we upturned the basin and the beans scattered over the concrete.

When we realised what we had done, we laughed, the two of us together. We were laughing at an old joke, a joke older than any palace, a cock's kidneys joke! And then we began, on hands and knees, to collect them. I think we lost only a few.

To be in the world is pain – the poem is true – and my hands tonight want to console you.

The poor are collectively unseizable. They are not only the majority on the planet, they are everywhere, and the smallest event somehow refers to them. Consequently the activity of the rich is the building of walls – walls of concrete, of electronic surveillance, of missile barrages, minefields, armed frontiers, media misinformation, and finally the wall of money to separate financial speculation from production. Only 3% of financial speculation and exchange concerns production. I love you.

Mi Guapo,

Did you receive the book by N.K.? I'm on the roof, the sun is going down and I have just talked on my mobile to our friends under mortar fire in Crocodilopolis. They tell jokes! Jokes.

I've threatened to tell you about angels. Angels once had wings. Some had twelve, others four, most had two. Angels were everywhere. There were one thousand five hundred and fifty myriad angels shouting and singing the praises of God. In addition there were the working angels. Every day of the week, every hour of the day, every cardinal point of the compass, every skill and occasion, every mountain and road, each had its angel. All the angels were born anew each morning.

I wonder what it felt like to be surrounded by such a dense population. Maybe like being born in a refugee camp!

Except that angels, for most of the time, were invisible. Invisible yet there – with their instructions, their opinions, their incessant voices, their wavebands.

Angiras in Sanskrit means divine spirit. Angaros in Persian means courier. *Angeles* in Greek means messenger.

Last week I saw Ved. He had drunk polluted water, and had a gastroenteritis with diarrhoea. I gave him some nifuroxazide (800 mg. per day) and some loperamide (12 mg. per day). And after he had pocketed the packets, he told me a story.

Gustavo, the shoemaker, is old and he dies. He dies in his shop whilst repairing a pair of sandals. An angel accompanies him to heaven. At one moment the angel speaks: If you want to, you can now look down, and you'll see the footprints of your life. The old man does so – and he sees the long trail of his steps. Yet something about what he sees puzzles him. Why is it, he asks, that two or three times, for quite a long way, my footprints stopped, as if my life had ended and I had died? How is it possible? And the angel laughs and replies: Those were the times I carried you!

Angels say things and sing, and all songs dream of being sung by an angel.

Maybe music and those angels with wings were twins, born one after the other. Music first. And if we want to imagine the loneliness of those moments before the first angel, when music was alone, listen to Billie Holliday!

They had their weaknesses too, the angels. In the fifteenth century it was calculated the number of fallen ones was 130 million! Many fell because, like Asael, they slept with a woman!

I'm not sure about the order here. It might have been the other way round – then the fall would come before, not afterwards. I'd never be tempted to accept an angel – but I can imagine accepting a fallen one!

Idelmis has moved her chair in the shop so she can see the ice-cream factory through the open door. She likes to see who's coming across the wasteland. She's now on the island of antalgics and antipyretics. She made a joke about this. She reads, ponders, dozes, and there are days when she gets up only once or twice to advise or serve a customer. Yet she chooses when to do this, for, at some level, she follows every transaction. Sometimes I think she's giving me my last lessons.

Night has fallen, there's a power cut, I can hear a drone surveying us from the sky, and I put my hands between yours before getting into bed with a candle.

Your A'ida

The Fear Industry. Last week the Salon du Bourget, international market showroom for weaponry, opened in Paris. One of the successful displays was of a white kiosk entitled Cogito 1002. Manufactured by SDS. In the box a traveller is seated, asked questions and obliged to place her/his hand on a surface operating as a biofeedback reader. The body's reactions to questions, as recorded by Cogito 1002, indicate whether or not the person is suspect. In use in US airports. Ready for export. If we could obtain a Cogito 1002 here we could play games with the herders – they'd be fascinated!

I'll tell you why I'm about to iron one of your shirts, the white one with darkish buttons, with four buttons on each cuff. You see the one I mean?

Last Friday it was cruelly hot. Over 40 Celsius. We were drinking water every half hour, and by the evening the sky was metallic and we were waiting for the storm. It took us by surprise. Maybe waiting for something doesn't lessen the surprise when it comes. It was as if everything that existed in the world had become rain.

I was still in the pharmacy, the noise on the roof was deafening. The noise of the heaviest rain is like the noise of fire, you told me once when we were crossing the Omar bridge.

I went to the door to look across the wasteland. Yellow rain was jumping up from the earth and grey rain sluicing down from the sky. Everything rain.

And I had an overwhelming desire to step into it, for it was immeasurable. We live each day with the immeasurable of one sort or another, no? I was thinking of you, so I did what I wanted. I stepped out into the deluge and shut the door behind me.

It wasn't like taking a shower, mi Soplete, it was instantaneous. The water took the whole of me and took my breath away at the same time. Probably I shrieked. I stayed there, no part spared, happy and limitless, like it was in the CAP 10B.

Someone shouted my name from far away. I could just

make out a man, holding a bag above his head, coming across the wasteland.

When he was an arm's length away, I saw who it was. Alexis. Alexis on one of his unannounced visits. He was as drenched as me and he was looking less happy. This made me pull him indoors.

We stood there, out of the downpour, dripping, dripping, making puddles on the tiled floor. We were amazed and we were about to laugh. We didn't laugh though, for we both had the same idea at the same moment.

We didn't say a word, and we began to bellow like elephants do, when they squirt water from their trunks and wash each other. We went on and on, exaggerating more and more crazily. Two elephants, using our left arms as trunks! And as we did this, the two of us, recalling our prison time, knew that along with the joke, what we were playing in was a dream of liberty! Yes, crazy. The craziness was the best part.

We turned our shoulders into elephants' ears to make you laugh, you, mi golondrino, and Murat and Durito and Ali and Silvio. You couldn't see us. We couldn't see you. You'd all been escorted back to your cells and banged up.

Hear them laughing! shouted Alexis.

I heard them.

The rain stopped, we made our way to the apartment. There we got ourselves dry and I lent Alexis this shirt of yours, a pair of trousers, some sandals. There was the chance of going to a Canasta Evening. It went well. Alexis won 3 black + 1 red. I said Acaba and asked permission to abandon. Next day, his clothes were dry and he went.

Now it's ironed, your shirt. I ironed it slowly. How many years since I ironed a shirt of yours? I know we count in days not years. I ironed it slowly and buttoned it right up to the collar. The buttons are the colour of dark slate. In the morning, from my pillow, I like to watch you standing there, at the foot of our bed, and you screw up your eyes and you have to undo three buttons before you can slip it over your head. Two thousand, one hundred and twenty-six days.

Your eternal A'ida.

Cam Yücel tells a story.

Yakov is a boy of seven and he asks his friend: how's it possible that men see everything with their eyes that are so small? They can see a whole city, take in a vast boulevard, how can all this fit into one small eye?

Well Yakov, I say, think of all the prisoners in this prison, a thousand of them. And think of their eyes grown huge with longing for the world outside. How is it, do you think, Yakov, that so many eyes are herded into such a small space?

Mi Soplete,

In the late autumns, during my childhood, my aunt Tania made a jam which she called Angels' Hair. It was made from large pumpkins and it tasted of toffee and parsnips. The flesh-coloured skins of the pumpkins were patterned with wisps and skeins, some red, some green, so they looked a bit like the head of an angel seen from behind. And I guess it was this which gave her jam its name. If I can find the recipe, I'll make some and send.

As it is, I send a sentence, written in the seventh century by Ibn Arabi. It was he who once remarked that the sight of God in woman was the most perfect of all! In the brig of Suse you would nearly all agree with that, no?

I found the sentence quoted in an article about Aristotle published in an old medical journal, which was used as wrapping round a box of syringes posted from Taiwan! The sentence says: Angels are the powers hidden in the faculties and organs of men.

I want to whisper to you, mi soplete, the questions and answers that come to me as I sit here alone – apart from Coing who is curled up in the chair she has taken over – night after night. I could say I'm sitting in your chair because you like to face the window when eating. Yet, we never had time enough to form real habits – except for sleeping in each other's arms. Yes, for this our bodies and our sleep had their habits. Something is pushing me.

A kind of amazement because fourteen centuries after that sentence was written, we can see why it is true.

I stare at this paper I'm writing on and I hear your voice. Voices are as different from each other as faces and far more difficult to define. How would I describe your voice to someone so they could infallibly recognise it? In your voice there's a waiting – like waiting for the train to slow down a little so you can jump. Even when you say: O.K., let's go, give me your hand, don't look back! Even then there's this quality of waiting in your voice. Or when you hold me in your arms on the hillside at Sevis and say: Stay here for ever!

Neurobiologists now know every living body consists – along with all its physical components and substances – of a ceaseless network of messages, and that these guide the activities of the body's cells so as to maintain, according to the circumstances, a maximum possible well-being and stability – what they call its homeostasis.

Another thing about your voice. When you speak your lips become like a curtain which is drawn back from your tongue and teeth, and the curtain is also a wound – which every time I want to put my mouth to.

The messages are delivered by ligands who travel vast distances along the bloodstream and along other channels. A ligand is a small molecule of amino acids. Hormones, peptides, steroids, neurotransmitters are all ligands. What makes the process hallucinatingly intricate and intimate is that each different kind of ligand has to find its own specific kind of receptor. Receptors are larger molecules of amino acids. On the surface of any single cell there may be hundreds of thousands of receptors. A single nerve cell has over a million – a million sticking-out ears awaiting, from the mouth of one of their own kind of ligands, a message, a message to be transmitted to the nucleus of the cell, so that it modifies its activities in the light of the news just received from the rest of the body and its surroundings.

When I write the word cell, I think of the one, numbered 73, which you are banged up in! Words never stop connecting one unlikely thing to another, and in this they are like our mothers. Mothers are always trying to bring everything together; they are the opposite of brigs! Which doesn't prevent some children being their mothers' lifelong prisoners.

Your voice has more 'S's in it than the average. It's sibilant, your missing voice. The voice I miss more than I can say.

The door to the pantry is open and on the left I can see the tap above the low-down sink, where I put the pots to water them. This evening when I came home I watered the two jasmines, the polyanthum and the yellow nudiflorum. You washed your feet there. Never in the basin next to the shower. Take off your sandals, wash one foot, tell me about your morning, then the second foot, tell me about your afternoon. Listening, I half imagine it's your ankle and the bones of your feet that are telling your hand what to tell to your voice to tell to me. And this is why I want to kiss each of those fifty-two bones of your two feet.

The messages delivered to the receptors range from the simplest indications – Forwards! Backwards! Open! Close! – to provoking highly complex codes of behaviour involving empathy, mutual aid, deceit, vengeance, self-sacrifice, caution, randiness.

How is it when, in the emptiness of the night, I say "I love you" I receive something immense? The silence is as total as before. It's not your response I've received. There was only my declaration. Yet I am fulfilled. Full of what? Why does an abdication become a gift to the one who abdicates? If we understood this, we'd have no more fear, Ya Nour. I love you.

The same ligands with their receptors are produced in body and brain, and operate as a network with the same authority in both. For them body and brain are equal. It's a long story. Certain ligands found in the human body are also found in [here the writing is illegible and blotted] one of the earliest living creatures to exist, mi soplete.

There are two ways in which ligands deliver their messages to their particular receptors. The most common is through a direct interlocking contact on the membrane surface of the cell – like you and a compañero tapping on the wall separating your two slots. In their case the message is an enzyme which transforms ATP into AMP which carries it further. Steroid ligands operate in another way; their receptors are not on the cell membrane but deep within its nucleus. So their information comes like a written message attached to a string dangled from a cell window on the floor above. The receptor delivers its message to the cell's DNA which sends it on further as an RNA. Sex hormones, for example, are steroid ligands. And my breasts are the shape they are thanks to the messages carried by gonadotrophine, oestrogen, progesterone and prolactin. They read a bit like the names of angels, no?

You have your own way, mi soplete, of reading. Sitting at this table reading the half-folded daily paper or lying on your back on our bed – your feet sticking out beyond the foot, holding the book with two hands above your face, maybe it's a book about mountain plants, the way you read, the way you perform the act of reading, is special. Some of us are drawn into the whirlpool of print, some of us take off on long flights, you assemble around you what you receive and immediately relate it to what's already here. When you're reading, far from being absent, you're more than ever present. I lie my head on your shoulder. Reading for you is a form of monitoring, and this is visible in the way you hold your chin. I turn my head which is resting on your shoulder and I put out my tongue to touch the underneath of your chin and then I raise my head a little and put my lips either side of where my tongue touched.

Messages received by receptors to which cells react, can slow down, accelerate, reverse, modify the workings of brain, glands, immune systems, spleen, gut and, equally, they provoke what we feel, how we desire, fear, run risks or hide.

Our bodies are made up of trillions of cells and their received messages form a network of ceaseless feedback and co-ordination. No high command, only a continual circuit of the body's own messengers, some of which existed since life began, and which, in their multiplicity, weave – that's the only word I can find – weave an intelligence comparable with the famous one of the mind. It looks as if body and mind are of the same substance. Angels are the powers hidden in the faculties and organs of men. And on the same page in the same journal from Taiwan, Aristotle called angels "intelligences".

Every cell is an individual – with its own birth date, lifetime and likely death date. Every cell has more or less a million receptors awaiting messages from ligands. Ligands were the first angels.

Why do I have to tell you this? Why is it so pressing? It's because of where we are, you and I.

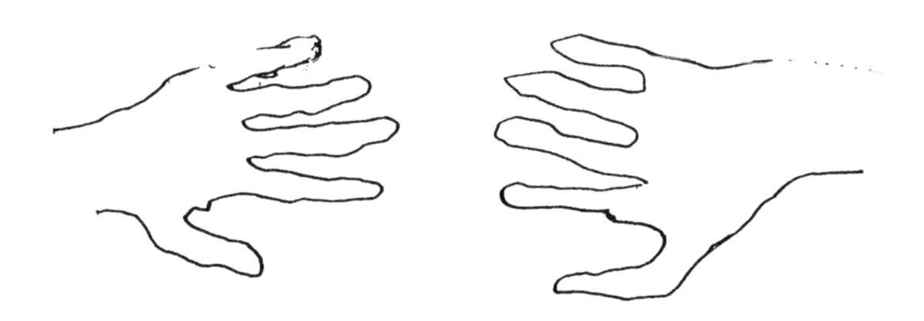

Neurobiology's discovery of ligand angels changes what we can guess about the mind. It also changes what's between the mind and the whole of nature which surrounds us. The view that the body is a physical machine directed by an immaterial, intangible mind, is finished. It lasted for only four centuries.

The mind is grounded in the body, through the mediation of the physical brain. The mind comes into being within and from nerve cells which are like every other living tissue. Mind and body, one insubstantial and the other substantial, are woven together into a single cloth, they are not two things, mi soplete, they are one thing.

You in your brig can't cover distances – except the repetitive minimal ones. Yet you think, and you think across the world. I can go where I want, covering distances is part of my life. Your thinking and my travelling, are almost the same thing. Thought and extension are parts of the same stuff. A single cloth.

With our minds you and I look for a way out of our days, which are often dark, trying to find that which is there, infinitely, in each minute!

This is why I have to tell it to you. Dreams in brigs often include angels. Angels are the polar opposite of herders – 'though there are good and bad in both camps. To be fully aware of angels you have to know what herders are. Outside prison, people forget the existence of both of them.

A mind is the consequence of the continual reading of events occurring in the body, and among those events are all the perceptions of the senses – what we see, hear, touch, smell, taste. I'm licking a spoonful of honey and drinking hot tea, it's cold tonight. You've buried your head under the blankets in your slot.

Today the first snow fell and the air was cold so it lined each bough, each branch, each twig of the fruit trees on our opposite hillside. Every detail of every tree was drawn in white. And tonight I send you this white tracery, as if it were an angel. What surrounds us is part of the same cloth too. Pull it over your head to keep warm with the words that come to me as I come to you.

The events of a body's perceptions, when read, become images in the mind. No mind, no images anywhere, my love.

The whole of nature is a telltale filter for the intelligence that has passed through it. Our bodies are part of the same filter, and from our bodies come our minds with which we read the tale. I'm taking my clothes off to tell you this.

A.

Irene. Good Night. In my dreams I get you . . .

Mi Guapo,

You are listening in your cell to my words as I write. I'm sitting up in bed. The pad is on my knees.

If I close my eyes I see your ears, the left one sticking out more than the right. My best friend at school used to claim that human ears are like dictionaries and that, if you know how, you can look up words in them. Limpid, for instance, Limpid.

My phone rang and there was Yasmina's clipped voice – finches chirp quickly like this when their tree is at risk – telling me that an Apache had been circling above the old tobacco factory in the Abor district, where seven of ours were hiding, and that the neighbouring women – and other women too – were preparing to form a human shield around the factory and on its roof, to prevent them shelling it. I told her I would come.

I put down the telephone and stood still, yet it was as if I was running. Cool air was striking my forehead. Something of mine – but not my body, maybe my name A'ida – was running, swerving, soaring, plummeting and becoming impossible to sight or get aim on. Perhaps a released bird has this sensation. A kind of limpidity.

I'm not going to send you this letter, yet I want to tell what we did the other day. Perhaps you won't read it until we are both dead, no, the dead don't read. The dead are what remains from what has been written. Much of what is written is reduced to ashes. The dead are all there in the words that stay.

By the time I got there, twenty women, waving white headscarves, were installed on the flat roof. The factory has three floors – like your prison. At ground level, lines of women with their backs to the wall, surrounded the entire building. No tanks, jeeps or Humvee yet to be seen. So I walked from the road across the wasteland to join them. Some of the women I recognised, others I didn't. We touched and looked at one another silently, to confirm what we shared, what we had in common. Our one chance was to become a single body for as long as we stood there and refused to budge.

We heard the Apache returning. It was flying slowly and low to frighten and observe us, its four-bladed rotor blackmailing the air below to hold it up. We heard the familiar Apache growl, the growl of them deciding and us rushing for shelter to hide – but not today. We could see the two Hellfire missiles tucked under its armpits. We could see the pilot and his gunner. We could see the mini-guns pointing at us.

Before the ruined mountain, before the abandoned factory, which was used as a makeshift hospital during the dysentery epidemic four years ago, some of us were likely to die. Each of us, I think, was frightened but not for herself.

Other women were hurrying down the zigzag path from the heights of Mount Abor. It's very steep there – you remember? – and they couldn't see the helicopter. They were holding on to each other and giggling nervously. It was strange to hear their laughter and the growling drone of the Apache together. I looked along the line of my companions, particularly at their foreheads, and I was convinced that some of them had felt something like I had. Their foreheads were limpid. When the stragglers from Mount Abor reached us, they adjusted their clothes and we warmly and solemnly embraced them.

The more we are, the larger the target we make, and the larger the target, the stronger we are. A weird, limpid logic! Each of us was frightened but not for herself.

The Apache was hovering above the factory roof, three floors higher in the sky, stationary but never still. We held one another's hands and from time to time repeated each other's names. I was holding the hands of Koto and Miriam. Koto was nineteen and had very white teeth. Miriam was a widow in her fifties whose husband had been killed twenty years ago. Although I'm not going to send you this letter I change their names.

At that moment we heard the tanks approaching down the street. Four of them. Koto was stroking my wrist with one of her fingers. We heard the tannoy voice announcing a curfew and ordering everyone to disperse and get indoors. The street on the other side of the wasteland was crowded, and I spotted several cameramen there. A few decigrams in our favour.

The immense tanks were now coming fast towards us, turrets turning to select their exact target.

The fear provoked by sounds is the hardest to control. The clatter of their tracks grappling and flattening whatever they drove over, the roar of their engines twisted into their suction noise, and the loudspeaker ordering us to disperse – all three becoming louder and louder, until they stopped in a line facing us, twelve metres away, and the muzzles of their 105 mm cannons even closer. We didn't huddle, we stood apart, only our hands touching. A commander emerging from the hatch of the first tank informed us, speaking our language badly, that we would now be forced to disperse.

Do you know how much an Apache costs? I asked Koto out of the corner of my mouth. She shook her head. Fifty million dollars, I said between my teeth. Miriam kissed my cheek. I was expecting the rear door of one of the tanks to be pushed up and the soldiers to emerge, land on their feet and round us up. It would have taken no more than a minute. And it didn't happen. Instead the tanks turned and, following each other with a distance of 20 metres between each, they began slowly to circle our circle.

I didn't think it then, mi Guapo, but now writing to you in the middle of the night, I think of Herodotus. Herodotus from Halicarnassus, who was the first to write down stories about tyrants being made deaf to every god by the din of their own machines.

We could never have resisted the soldiers, they would have carted us off. The tanks, as they circled us, deliberately drew nearer – they were tightening the noose slowly around us.

You know how a cat measures her jump, the distance of it, landing on her four feet close together, on the very spot she calculated? This is what each of us had to do, measuring, not the distance of a leap, but its opposite – the precise amount of willpower needed to take the terrifying decision to stay put, to do nothing, despite fear. Nothing. If you underestimated the willpower needed, you'd break line and run before you realised what you were doing. The fear was constant but it fluctuated. If you overestimated, you'd be exhausted and useless before the end and the others would have to prop you up. Our holding hands helped because the calculating energy passed from hand to hand.

When the tanks had circled the factory once, they were no more than an arm's length away from us. Through the netted vents of their hulls, we could see helmets, eyes, gloved hands.

More terrifying than anything else was the armoured plating, seen so close up! When each tank passed, it was this surface, the most impermeable ever created by man, that we couldn't avoid seeing, even if we sang – and we had now started singing – with its rounded blind rivets, its texture of an animal hide so it never shines, its granite hardness and its shit colouring, the colouring not of a mineral but of decay. It was against this surface that we were waiting to be crushed. And facing this surface we must decide, second by second, not to move, not to budge.

My brother, shouted Koto, my brother says any tank can be destroyed if you find the right place and the right moment!

How were we able – all three hundred of us – to hold

out as we did? The caterpillar treads were now a few centimetres from our sandals. We didn't move. We went on holding hands and singing to each other in our old women's voices. For this is what had happened and this is why we could do what we did. We had not aged, we were simply old, a thousand years old.

A long burst from a machine gun in the street. Positioned as we were, we couldn't see properly what was happening, so we made signs to our old sisters on the roof who could see better than us. The Apache hung menacingly above them. They made signs back and we understood that a patrol had fired on some running figures. Soon we heard the wail of a siren.

The suction of the next tank hemming us in, ruffled and billowed our skirts. Do nothing. We didn't budge. We were terrified. And in our shrill grandmother's voices, we were singing – We're here to stay! Each of us armed with nothing except a derelict uterus.

That's how it was.

Then one tank – we didn't immediately believe our dim eyes – stopped circling and headed off across the wasteland, followed by the next and the next and the next. The old women on the roof cheered, and we, still holding hands but now silent, began to side-step towards the left so that slowly, very slowly as befitted our years, we were circling the factory.

About an hour later, the seven were ready to slip away. We, their grandmothers, dispersed, remembering what it had been like to be young and then becoming young. And within ten minutes I heard the news, passed from mouth to mouth: Manda, the music teacher, had been shot dead in the street. She was trying to join us.

The lute is like no other instrument, she used to say, as soon as you balance a lute on your lap, it becomes a man! Manda!

For so long as I am alive, I am yours, mi Guapo.

[Letter unsent]

Ya Nour,

Each new death prepares us for something – of course for our own deaths – mine not yours, nothing could prepare me for yours, I'll sit on the earth, your head in my lap, their cluster bombs exploding, and I will refuse your death. Each new death also prepares us for a carnival, a carnival held under their very noses, and about which they can do fuck all, not even with their Predator Drones. I'm thinking of how they shot Manda.

At her burial we were several hundred, and afterwards we sang a few, only a few, of her songs, and they were a rehearsal for the carnival they are shit-scared of.

There isn't a song in the world which isn't in part addressed to the dead, and the dead pocket the songs, put them in their pocket of silence, their front pocket of silence, with the key of the house, an identity card, a few of their bank notes and a knife. I have a new knife, mi Kadima, given me by Soko.

Or rather, it's not new, she found it on the ground and was too superstitious to keep it. So she gave it to me, saying: I swear to God you're the only one I know who will never, I'm certain, never slit her own throat!

I use it for chopping mint and cutting pineapples. It has a bone handle and a sheath. If necessary, I could stab with it.

The dead put our songs into their pocket of silence and then the silence changes, it's no longer one of distance but of closeness, a shared silence. Like the one between Amitara and Victor and Yaha and Emil and Zakaria and Susan and Naci and Valentina and César being shared with you and me, who are still alive. Like the silence tonight between Manda and myself.

In a main square a large clock on the roof of the town hall told the time. Whenever a train from the country arrived – once a day very early in the morning – there was a smart man standing in the square comparing the clock's time with that of his own pocket watch. A shepherd, who had just arrived by train in the town, looking for work, asked the man what he was doing standing there for so long? I'm waiting, the man explained, this is one of my jobs, checking the town clock. When the big clock stops, I have here – he pointed at his watch – I have here the right time, so the town clerk can reset the town hall clock correctly. Does it stop often? Several times a week, and when it stops, they consult me, and I tell them the proper time, and they pay me. They pay me almost a dollar!! Easy money! To tell the truth I have many jobs to do, too many. Look – I like your face, if you want I'll pass this one on to you. You can have the watch – it goes with the job – for just half a dollar!

I hear Manda's deep voice telling the story. In another life she was called Sevgi. She could tell stories like a man does, like a woman does, or like a child can. It all depended on the story. I see the square with cobbles. I see the shepherd's face. He's going to say: Fine! I'll pay on the first day the Big Clock stops!

When they shot Manda down in the Mount Abor district, they shot her down in every one of her stories. And her blood is on the cobbles in the square where the shepherd outwitted the smart man. When there's nobody asking for advice or a medicine in the pharmacy, I find myself talking to her silence.

This evening on my windowsill when I got home, there was a tumbler with pink jelly in it, and embedded in the jelly, sliced strawberries and bananas.

Ama's room is very small, so when she cooks she put her gas burner outside her door on the roof, and with the door open she can survey it, sitting on her bed! On the burner there's space for two saucepans. She cooks at odd hours. She must have made the strawberry jelly this morning.

When I buy baklava, which is not often because I eat too many, I leave a few for her on her windowsill, with a head scarf over them so the wasps don't come. For these little gifts we don't thank each other with words. They are commas of care.

One evening a week ago a kid came into the pharmacy and asked whether I'd seen a ginger cat during the last twenty-four hours, answering to the name of Fox. I said,

No, we've seen no cat. I didn't recognise the kid, maybe he was seventeen years old. It was easy to picture him with a gun but that evening he was unarmed. He had very dark eyes, black sideburns, and a narrow moustache. A lithe body. The last time we saw the cat, he said, she was scared and running across the wasteland here towards the ice-cream factory. I nodded.

If you see her and can catch her, he said, good, if not and you see her, can you phone me – here's my cell phone number. He gave me a scrap of paper on which he'd already written it. Is she yours? I asked him. He looked at me as if I should know better.

She belongs to Gema, he said, who's ninety and lives by herself. I'm scared for Gema if she doesn't find her cat. Last night she couldn't sleep. She calls her Fox because of her colour.

I'll keep a lookout, I told him and then his eyes caught mine and I guessed we were both of us wondering about the same thing – about living to be ninety!

Thanks, he said, thanks a lot.

Commas of care! Punctuating days with them is something long-term prisoners learn, isn't it? But after days of not writing to you, and weeks without a letter from you, commas are not enough! I need two lines of a song – a song sung before any fucking commas or writing on paper existed!

My desire is my mascara
When I see you, my eyes shine!

Your A.

We heard about the paintings of Htein Lin who served nearly seven years in the prisons of Myanmar. He painted on the washed white cotton of discarded prison shirts. Nothing else available. He also made sculptures out of bars of regulation prison soap. He was released from Myaungmya Jail in 2004. Maybe he could send a painting to us, we wondered. And it happened.

Durito takes it, folded, out of his pocket. We watch. He unfolds it. Holds it before us like a toreador's cape. Except it's thin, sparse, whitish cotton, and would barely be large enough to cover a man's torso. On to the cotton is painted a circle which fits into a painted stand, like a globe of the world in a classroom, or like a round mirror on a dressing table.

In the circle is painted a man's boot. Right foot. The colours were applied through syringes and rubbed in with the fingers. For black he used vinyl house paint. The laces of the boot are loose and the tongue is hanging out. A painted bunch of stalks, like cuttings from a fruit or olive tree, have been placed in the painted boot, and at the end of each stalk there is a painted clock-face instead of a blossom.

The clock faces are different sizes: some no bigger than a wrist-watch, others as big as an old fashioned alarm clock with a bell at the top. The time according to any one of the clocks is difficult to read and it looks as if each dial announces a different time. Probably some are am.; others pm. What's clear is that there are a dozen or more different times, and that they are irreconcilable.

Each of us recognises because of this how Htein Lin is an experienced prisoner. We decide to take his painting to our cells in turn. Fold it, pocket it, unfold it, remove our own boots, think of other times. And next day hand the folded painted cotton on to another compañero.

Mi Soplete,

The temperature didn't fall during the night (41 Celsius) and this morning in the pharmacy it was stifling. To make matters worse, there was a power cut and so no fan. Sometimes it feels as if they have taken over even the seasons – particularly during daylight hours. (At night they are more frightened than we.)

I went to visit Soko. It was for the first time since, poor Soko, she lost her husband, and I was surprised because now she complains about nothing. Odd, isn't it, how loss can precipitate crystals of courage?

Soko, who never stopped lamenting and begging God to take her to heaven, has become stoic. Can it be a question of having nothing more to lose? I'm not so sure. Her nephew, who disappeared five years ago, has surfaced in London where he has found work as a plumber. He was trained as a lawyer and went into hiding after the AI radio was shut down. She says he met you once.

Despite her cataracts, she is still dressmaking. Without money, she repeats, there's nothing, nothing. But now she says this with another intonation, as if the observation itself clarified the solution.

She insists that we eat an apricot tart she has made. From dried apricots.

The power is still cut, and the two candles in their sticks on her table are almost burnt out. Wait, she says, I have some. She looks in a drawer and comes back holding two new candles.

She melts the bottom of one with the flame guttering in the hole of the candlestick and pushes it down firmly. Is it vertical? she asks. I can't see, tell me, is it vertical? It was always Alex who fixed the new candles, she explains. Is it vertical? she asks again. If it is not, it drips.

A little to the right, I tell her, perfect now.

She places the second candle. You're sure it's vertical? I nod. If it is not, it drips. Perfect I say. Alex had a sharp eye for the upright! she says, and he always took his time, to plant candles properly.

And suddenly I find myself shouting her name Soko! and weeping.

I couldn't eat the tart, I couldn't explain. I was dead tired and she told me to lie down on the divan, which I did.

We forget fatigue, mi Soplete, and fatigue is as patient as Alex was with the candles. Fatigue waits and is like rust. It eats into the strongest wills, turns into red dust the most fervent hopes, undermines our energies. Fatigue wants to put an end to the endless putting off and putting off. It choses finally the shorter answer. Most of all, fatigue opts for quiet, not caring any more that it's the quiet of the dead.

At some point when tending someone you love who is in pain, you reach the edge of a lake, and you look at each other with such joy at the stillness.

[Letter unsent]

Mi Golondrino,

Two winters ago I think it was, I mentioned a man to you, a diabetic who came one night to the pharmacy in urgent need of sugar. Did I tell you? He was beside himself, but as chance would have it, I happened to be there. I gave him what he needed and he left. He spoke with an accent and I didn't ask him where he was from and he didn't give me his name. Because I talk to you so often in my head, I sometimes get muddled about what I've put or haven't put into my letters. In a city without prisons – has there ever been one? – who would ever guess one can put so much into letters?

I reread your letters many times. Not at night. Rereading them then tends to be dangerous for the night. I read them in the morning after coffee and before work. I go outside so I can see the sky and the horizons. Often I go up onto the roof. At other times I go outside, cross the road and sit on the fallen tree, where the ants are. Yes, still. I take your letter out of its soiled envelope and I read. And as I read the days between clatter past like the freight wagons of a train! And what do I mean by the days between? Between this time and the last time I read the same letter. And between the day you wrote it and the day they took you. And between the day one of the herders posted it and the day I'm sitting on the roof reading it. And between this day when we have to remember everything and the day when we'll be able to forget because we have all. These, my love, are the days between, and the closest railway to here is two hundred kilometres away.

This morning I was in your Suse buying a new pack of cards. I was crossing the market where the orange stalls are, and a man steps from behind me and says:

I owe you a word of thanks.

Thanks? Why?

Two years ago in Sucrat you saved my life.

How come?

A shot of sugar.

You mean sugar or an amphetamine?

Late one night.

It was then I remembered him and his weighed-down shoulders and his curious accent and his anger, his anger that had signalled how low his sugar-count probably was. He was the man I think I told you about who came that night to the pharmacy.

I'm living in the next street, behind the barber's, he says, please be my guest so I can offer you a coffee. It's two years I've been waiting.

I don't have much time.

I work as a cleaner in the market and I have to begin in an hour, so a quick coffee.

If you wish.

We went down a narrow passageway beside the barber's.

There, he says, nodding to the men having their hair cut and being shaved – more truths come out there than in most prayers!

You've been working in the market for long?

Five years, ever since I took the decision to follow my vocation.

Vocation?

By way of reply, he unlocks a front door, which opens outward and extends his arm in a gesture of invitation for me to enter.

It's bare, but I beg you make yourself at home. Italian coffee or Turkish?

Whichever is easiest.

It's simply a question of how I grind it.

He disappeared into a kind of closet which gave on to a corner of the room, and plugged in a coffee grinder. An aroma of coffee as astringent as resin, filled the room.

The room was small. It must have been a small shop. Perhaps a haberdasher's. There was a tight, neat roll of bedding on the floor against one wall, a large table before a window, and two stools. Nothing else. No curtains, no rugs, no pictures, no overhead lighting. A reading lamp on the table.

Your coffee smells good.

You can judge, my honourable guest, when you've tasted it.

May I ask about your vocation?

My vocation, he replied standing in the doorway of the closet, was to be a poet.

Was?

It was settled long before I knew it. It took me thirty years to figure it out. Before that I sold carpets. It's still my vocation, needless to say, if you wish you can look on my table.

On the long table in front of the window, a dozen sheets of paper, the same size, and carefully aligned – like stepping stones – were laid out from left to right. Each one was covered with a small neat handwriting, frequently corrected or crossed-out. Beside certain passages a large question mark had been pencilled in; occasionally beside a passage there was a tick.

The regular left margin of each page and the differing lengths of the short lines showed it was being written as poetry. Several other sheets covered with the same close writing waited on the windowsill. I couldn't read a single word. It looked like Turkish. I asked him.

Yes and no. I write in the language of the Taurus mountains, this is my mother tongue. She's alone all day and wants to hear stories in the evening.

He gave me a special look as if he was checking to make sure that I recognised how things were not as they seemed to be. Certain beggars do the same after being given alms: their look says – thank me for having chosen you!

I went over to see what he was doing in the closet. The coffee in the copper pot had risen twice and he was adding the last spoonful of cold water. Wherever there was a space on a horizontal surface in the closet – near the gas-ring, beside the basin, under the mirror – there were single sheets of paper covered with the same meticulous handwriting. He watched me noticing this.

I move around when I'm working, particularly in the early morning before the sun's up. If it doesn't come to me by the big table, I take a stool and sit by the front door or I wander out here to eat some bread or brush my teeth.

I move around from valley to valley, from Mount Ararat to the Heights of Goksul or to the Passes of Cilicie.

Again he gave me the beggar look.

Then he handed me my cup of coffee. I sipped. It was the best I'd tasted for a long while. I installed myself on one of the stools near the table.

Is it one long poem?

Maybe no poet writes more than one and it takes a lifetime. He thinks he's writing different short poems but really they're all part of the same long one.

What's it about?

It's in praise of life and its abundance. When I'm sweeping in the market, I listen, I never stop listening and often the words I hear are so well chosen, I remember them. A question of keeping your ears open – diabetics, as you must know, run a higher risk than most of becoming both deaf and blind.

You could translate a line or two for me? I ask.

The coffee pleases you?

It's remarkable.

You can still taste it between your eyes forty minutes after you've drunk it – provided everything else is calm. Yesterday we had a rocket from one of their Apaches.

A few lines?

I wanted to offer you a coffee and show you my secret because I think you saved my life.

A few lines?

I'll read you some lines then without translating. You'll hear the secret and it'll still be a secret.

The sound of his voice in the room changed, and it was

as if we were sitting under a tree. I let the words pass without asking anything of them. Then he said:
We tend to think secrets are small, no? like precious jewels or sharp stones or knives that can be hidden and kept secret because they're small. But there are also secrets which are huge, and it is because of their immensity that they remain hidden except to those who have tried to put their arms around them. These secrets are promises.

He gave me another beggar look.

I drank the last dregs of the delicious coffee, I thanked him, and, as I was leaving, he pronounced his name for the first time: Hasan.

Writing this to you late tonight. I think of your letters which I reread early in the mornings when the days between clatter past like freight wagons, and I think of my letters that you read in your cell, and I smile at their immense secret which is ours, yours and mine.

This morning the temperature was several degrees below zero and Silvio found a white kitten in the dark corner of the Exercise Yard. At first, he said, he thought it was a handful of snow. Nobody knows how it got there. Probably fell from the roof of the mirador, but how did it get there? Lying immobile in the corner on the asphalt. Silvio stooped to examine it more closely. The herder hurried forward targeting him with his Uzi 5. S. straightened up, continued walking and negotiated. He insisted on the fact that Kadem is a veterinary surgeon. The herder consulted his on-board data cell phone. After a quarter of an hour it was agreed S. would deposit the kitten in the Common Room. Kadem examined her and announced there was nothing to be done, her back was broken, and, if he could but he couldn't, he'd give her an injection. He laid her on a blanket near the stove. Her white mouth was slightly open and her tongue was scarcely less white than her teeth. From time to time she exhaled as if hissing, her eyes were open. Then she rolled on to her side and extended all four legs, her hind legs straight out behind her, as if she were about to leap, and her forelegs before her. Everyone was watching in silence. With her two front paws she wiped her face, beginning with the ears down to the white mouth, over the eyes. She wiped her eyes as if wiping away the illusions of life, and this done, she was dead. Nobody spoke. The two herders had become suspicious, pacing around, bolting and unbolting their guns. Kadem nodded smiling, and picked the kitten up in the blanket. Nobody spoke. Each of us silent, Kadem murmured. like the thief the dog bit.

She had escaped.

Mi Guapo,

I have a memory from very long ago, so long ago I'm not sure whether it belongs to my childhood or what I heard from others when I was a child. Sometimes your old woman wonders, mi Guapo, whether all childhood memories are not partly hearsay? As a child you're learning so much so quickly that you forget where a piece of news first came from. When did I first take in death? Was it my discovery or did somebody solemnly talk to me. How did I learn that water always tries to go lower? I first found this out for myself.

I have a memory which I want to share with you. It's about a secret practice of women, men, old people, children. We become aware of this practice obliquely, it's not something we're looking for, and very quickly we take it for granted.

Watch trees and see how they move in the wind. Watch animals and notice how cautiously yet independently they go their separate ways – running, burrowing, ambling, flying. The same for fishes and their way of swimming! I want to make you smile in 73. The smile you have when you've hit upon an idea of how to repair something but haven't yet checked it out. Your half-hidden smile.

Now consider human lives, their every-minute, everyday lives! Their lives depend upon an agreed regularity to which each contributes. Maintaining this regularity is the forgotten practice I'm talking about.

It explains the arrival of the fruit in the market each day, the lights in the street at night, the letters slipped under the front door, the matches in a match box all pointing in the same direction, music heard on the radio, smiles exchanged between strangers. The regularity has a beat, very distant, often inaudible, and at the same time similar to a heartbeat.

No place for illusions here. The beat doesn't stop solitude, it doesn't cure pain, you can't telephone it – it's simply a reminder that you belong to a shared story.

And in our life today we are condemned to endless irregularity. Those who impose this on us are frightened by our irregularity. So they build walls to keep us out. Yet their walls will never be long enough and there'll always be ways round, over and under them.

'Till soon. Your A'ida.

When I think now about what we were doing twenty years ago, I'm struck by the precariousness of our situation then, a precariousness which we, engaged in our struggle, mostly ignored or didn't see. And this is strangely reassuring in face of what we are up against today, for it suggests precariousness is our strength.

Mi Guapo,

Thank you for the orchard of jasmine you somehow sent. I lie down in that orchard.

When I was taking my shower an idea came into my head: every pain slides, at one, point, into the word NO, before continuing on its way. Just as every pleasure slides into the word YES before continuing!

To you I say YES; to the life we are having to live I say NO. Yet I am proud of that life, proud of what we have done, proud of us. And when I think this, I become a third person, neither you nor I, and you become the same third person – beyond any yes or no!

Today because it's my birthday I keep repeating YES. I look at myself in the mirror. I'm standing, my hair is loose, and I say yes. I notice the tenderness of my skin and the blackness of my hairs and I say yes. I remember reading how the lover compares the upper part of his beloved's body to camphor, the middle to amber, and the lower part to musk, and I say yes.

My limbs long to be seen by you not by me. There are moments when they are angry with me for this. They insinuate – moving sinuously – they insinuate it's my fault you are not with them, and the more they move when they're in this mood, the more they insist they cannot forgive me, will never forgive! And who do you think you are? I ask them in anger. We are happiness, they reply.

I shut my eyes and I tell them to remember prison and what it's like pacing, sitting, standing still, hunching over, sleeping in a cell. And for a moment they recall it with me. In prison the body is stripped of its kingdom. Like every other personal effect it is confiscated on entry. And on discharge, when the wristwatch, the bracelets, the wallet, the nail-file are handed back, the kingdom is missing and has to be slowly refound, province by province.

I open my eyes and again look in the mirror. Because they are not in prison, my limbs want to entice you and offer you their happiness.

Yes, yes, yes, yes. Each yes is a dish I'm going to prepare for the friends I've invited. I will chop up vegetables, skewer meat, make batter, beat eggs, crush chickpeas, prepare the mixture for pancakes, peel cloves of garlic, cut mint, shake the molokhiyya. I want my guests to believe all the dishes came down, full, from heaven, Yes.

Many dishes, many yeses, like this I will smile with confidence tonight when they ask me about you, and I'll think of the hoopoe, who brought news from the Queen of Sheba, and who builds her nests in ruins.

Yes, the sun is up and the wind has just got up, which makes three of us. See, my love, the eucalyptus on the far side of the quadrant? If I stand on tiptoe in the front doorway, I'm dressed at last and I'm wearing a long, billowing whitish skirt, I can watch it, it's leaning over, far over, with the fierce wind, and is almost dancing! Its bark still falls off in those long curved pieces which you said you could make a canoe out of. I was wrong. The eucalyptus is dancing! Sails unfurled from her green branches, whole continents of leaves dancing to the sway of the most womanly of women. Such a joy. Ukulele eucalyptus. What hips! My birthday.

Later, whilst preparing our feast, I myself dance, between sweeping the floor and putting the tablecloths on and placing the benches and rolling out pastry and cooking mushrooms and slicing up pineapples whilst leaving their coats on, and arranging flowers and turning meat and polishing glasses, I dance. Yes, yes, yes, . . . many friends are coming.

Now the last guest has gone and your orchard of jasmine on the windowsill is already predicting the first light. The birds outside are singing at their loudest. They are filling the silence, the silence the dead leave behind. Often unbearable that silence. The silence of Amitara, Zakaria, Susan, Victor, Emil, Yaha, César.

Yet this silence is lined, I promise you, it is lined with tenderness. And if you doubt this, remember touching with your finger the inside of one of the nests the birds are building. Such softness and tenderness is the result of endless forays and skirmishes, and also of a cunning, learnt through the ages, of constructing only with what is pliable, resistant, and strong. Touch one . . .

I wait a moment to touch you. Then we'll sleep. Sleep is the first house, house without roof, walls or bed. They came later, inspired by sleep. Tonight, the night after my birthday, I'm taking you, my love, into the first house. I slip it under the monstrous door and you'll find me inside it.

Your A'ida.

Ya Nour,

Sleep is the first house, house without roof, walls or bed. They came later, inspired by sleep. Tonight I'm taking you, my love, into the first house. I slip it under the monstrous door and you'll find me inside it.

Tonight your A'ida

Exit tonight.

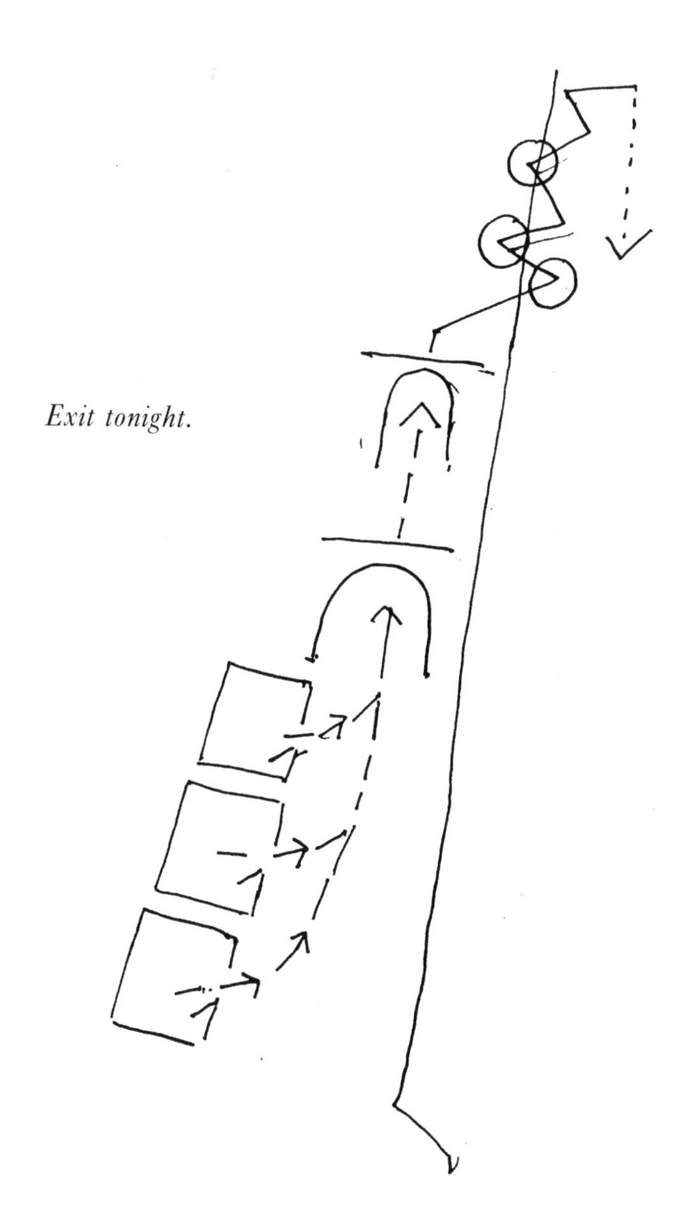

Acknowledgements

Nobody knows how a book comes about, but one can name precisely some of those who were essential to this mysterious process. In this case:

Alex, Anne, Beverly, Charline, Elia, Gareth, Guy, Hans, Iona, Irene, Isabel, Jean-Pierre, Jeremy, Kamal, Katya, Latife, Leila, Mahmoud Maria M., Maria N., Michael, Michel D., Michel R., Nacho, Nella, Omar, Petra, Pilar, Ramón, Rema, Sandra, Selçuk, Tania, Tom, Yasmina, Yves, Yvonne, Ziad. Thank you.

Printed in the United States
By Bookmasters